Praise for *Serious Girls* by **P9-DFO-847**

"Poetic."

—*Seventeen*

"A compelling Swann dive into the psyches of boarding school girls."
—*New York* magazine

"Swann's promising debut is a delicate, clear-eyed distillation of teenage girls' greatest concerns: identity, authenticity, and sexual power. . . . *Serious Girls* palpably evokes the frustration and anxiety of growing up."

—*Entertainment Weekly*

"Writing in compressed, staccato prose, Swann deftly evokes the narrator's febrile, gauze-cloaked consciousness. . . . It is not the Brontës she recalls but Albert Camus's *The Stranger*."

—*Time Out*

"*Serious Girls* is a commanding debut from this soon-to-be well-known writer . . . a masterpiece in the making: a thoughtful, insightful piece of literature that will hopefully be read voraciously by many."
—*King Features Weekly Service*

"With sensitivity and quiet wit, O. Henry Award–winner Swann delineates the turmoil of adolescence. . . . Wonderfully perceptive and precise about an age that's too often portrayed in vague generalities."
—*Kirkus Reviews*

"Maxine Swann's novel is a small masterpiece. Entirely original, it combines Proust's attention to the inner life, Colette's understanding of the body, and Jean Rhys's knowledge of the dangers of love."
—Mary Gordon, author of *Spending*

"Mysteriously, magically, Maxine Swann seems to know both the secrets of adolescence and of writing a wonderful novel. I don't know when I last read a book that so beautifully conveys the intense yearnings of that period between childhood and adulthood. *Serious Girls* is an exhilarating debut."

—Margot Livesey, author of *Eva Moves the Furniture*

SERIOUS GIRLS

MAXINE SWANN

PICADOR   NEW YORK

www.picadorusa.com

Picador® is a U.S. registered trademark and is used by St. Martin's Press under license from Pan Books Limited.

For information on Picador Reading Group Guides, as well as ordering, please contact the Trade Marketing department at St. Martin's Press.
Phone: 1-800-221-7945 extension 763
Fax: 212-677-7456
E-mail: trademarketing@stmartins.com

Library of Congress Cataloging-in-Publication Data

Swann, Maxine.
    Serious girls / Maxine Swann.
        p. cm.
    ISBN 0-312-28802-6 (hc)
    ISBN 0-312-28801-8 (pbk)
    EAN 978-0312-28801-3
    1. Teenage girls—Fiction. 2. Female friendship—Fiction. 3. Boarding school—Fiction. I. Title.

PS3619.W356S47 2003
813'.6—dc21
                                   2003053600

First Picador Paperback Edition: December 2004

10 9 8 7 6 5 4 3 2 1

For Juan Pablo

SERIOUS GIRLS

CHAPTER I

IT WAS NOT THAT I MISSED HOME, THOUGH I WOULD SOMEtimes remember things. As I was walking along the stone paths back to the dormitory or lying on my bed in the afternoons, I'd suddenly think of lying on the great shards of stone by the creek, the shadows of the leaves moving over my skin. Or I'd remember standing up in one of the fruit trees while my mother worked in her garden nearby. I remembered how she worked, always calmly, never still, and how I loved to watch her hands. They were strong and nicely shaped and, in the summer, turned very brown. When she wasn't working in other people's gardens, or, in winter, in the greenhouses of the farms, she usually worked in her own. She cut back the briars at the edge of the yard or pruned the trees. She wouldn't notice me. Her eyes, graygreen, had a dimness in them as if she was always looking far away. So, although her face was very pretty—everyone said so—I preferred to look at her hands. Or else I'd think of Jasper. I actually spent most of my time with him, out in the woods or in his rooms above the barn. I'd climb the stairs and knock. He'd have the music on, and the woodstove burning in winter and the fans blowing in summer. "Listen to this," he'd say, right away, when I came in—he always had a new story to tell. I'd remember these things, and remember, too, the note my grandmother had sent. I'd come upon it, open on my mother's desk—"I've stayed out of it until now, as you wished," she wrote, "I only request this one thing"—offering to send me away to school. "Otherwise she'll be stunted," she went on, "living out there in the boondocks. I remember distinctly that blank look she had."

It was like beginning all over again.

My room at boarding school was in a white clapboard house with shutters. Nine other girls lived there. The furniture, I'd noticed that first day, was out of proportion, the bed short and narrow, the bureau and the desk very large. On the ceiling there was a light fixture, a mixture of flowers and yellow-green vines, each flower holding a bulb.

In the afternoons, the dormitory was nearly always empty. The halls were quiet. The stretches of grass outside were quiet. Lying there sometimes in the emptiness and silence, I was free to imagine myself as a leaf whose stem had snapped, drifting over water, passing here a set of ripples, there a bright shining pool.

Mornings were different, clamorous, frightening. The girls clattered back and forth along the hall, up and down the wooden stairs. They shrieked and laughed and slammed their doors. I put on my uniform, a stiff tunic, cobalt blue, with a white collared blouse underneath, and sat down on the bed to wait. Once they were all gone, I crept out.

The dim bathroom at the end of the hall had one window, high up, yellowed over. There were two sinks and a mirror spotted with bronze and silver spots. I looked in it. Someone knocked. I didn't answer. There was a second knock, more tentative.

"Who is it?" I asked.

It was the small girl with freckles who lived two doors down. She must have waited, too. I saw her once whispering to herself out on the path. When she looked up, she blushed. There, I thought, she's afraid, too. But I still couldn't bring myself to speak to her.

Outside, the warm brick of the buildings, the cool stone paths. At first I felt bewildered and kept getting lost. Everything, paths and buildings, looked exactly the same. Then, quite quickly, I latched on to things, a set of astonishingly cragged fruit trees outside the dining hall, a moss-covered wall lining the road. One day I discovered a stone bench along the side of the chapel. Out in front of the chapel was a wide stretch of grass, the Green, it was called. This was where the girls gathered in the afternoons. Some huddled and talked. Others had hockey sticks and hit a ball around. I watched them from the bench. There were different kinds of girls, I understood this quickly. At one end of the spectrum were the smooth popular ones; at the other, the outcasts. Between them existed a larger middle ground where all the others lingered, anxious about their fate, drifting at times toward the one extreme, at times toward the other.

One day, as I was sitting on the bench, I saw the history teacher, Mr. Ryan, pass by, walking with the French teacher, Madame Loup. He's in love with her, I thought. How could he not be?

Madame Loup. Her classroom was on an upper floor. It had tall windows that looked out over the school pond, and a pale blue carpet smelling faintly of smoke. Before we saw her, we heard the click of her heels. And then her voice in the hall, laughing or shouting something over her shoulder at someone. When she entered, it was always, it seemed, with surprise—to find us there, to be there herself. Her eyes were large and brown, with a darker brown rim. They drooped in general but widened at the sight of us. She had a high straight nose and a deeply carved mouth. She made a joke, or one of her favorite students in the front made a joke, and her deeply carved mouth opened in a flash, revealing long teeth, somewhat stained, as she laughed.

Then, fluffy bronze hair falling in her eyes, she clicked her wobbly way into the room. Her clothes were wonderful, small buttoned coats and fitted skirts the same color, often brown, the cuffs and hems rimmed in fur. Carelessly, sprawling, she dropped her things on the desk, as if entering her own bedroom at home. Then she sat down, slouched in her chair, peered out at us, and finally began. In her murmuring, heavily accented voice, she told us something, usually something that had happened to her in the past day, which she linked with something else, a scene or character from a book—for example, a woman in a shop in town who behaved like a character in Flaubert—and so on for the opening speech of the day. All this was in English. Although she was supposed to be teaching us French, that was clearly not what interested her. Each day she had a student present the grammar lesson to the class. Usually she'd pay a kind of mild attention. But she always had her own papers before her on the desk, piles of stiff, stained pages filled with spidery script that she'd peer at over glasses as the lesson was presented, looking up at the speaking student now and then, nodding and smiling vaguely and looking back down.

Then, abruptly, out of what seemed either irritation or inspiration, she'd stand, announcing that this would be all of the lesson for the day. The student would, in most cases, happily retreat. Madame Loup would walk to the window and stand there, one elbow up, hand poised before her face—even when she wasn't smoking, she made the gestures of smoking—and think for a moment, the daylight on her face making her look suddenly old. She'd pause and then turn and speak rapturously for the rest of the hour about Virginia Woolf or Proust or Sylvia Plath.

Though none could compare with Madame Loup, my other teachers were also a source of intense curiosity. Mr. Ryan, who taught us European history, was small but perfectly proportioned. He was quick, quick-moving, quick-witted. Occasionally he got impatient and enraged and walked out of the classroom, slamming the door, and then, after a moment or two, came back in, smiling at and mimicking himself. This was his more usual expression of frustration, mimicry, and he did it extremely well, mimicking girls' expressions or postures when they were searching for an answer or hadn't done their homework. He was said to be a reformed alcoholic with a dark past. This only added glamour to his appeal (I'd heard the girls whispering) and seemed to suggest that despite his present situation—he had a wife and three small children and lived just below us on the first floor of the dormitory—he could at any moment slip back into reckless behavior of all kinds.

Sometimes, walking along and thinking of all this—Madame Loup, the Wars of the Roses, the poems of Sylvia Plath—I would feel as if my brain were flowering.

There was that flowering feeling, the feelings of fear, the emptiness and silence of the afternoons.

The sky in the winter could have a dull gray look. But softer when it snowed. My mother didn't like winter because she hated to stay indoors, but she liked the snow. When it first arrived, she and her boyfriend would take me out to play in it. When we played out in the snow together after school, I'd forget about the purple-black look the sky could also have and about what the neighbor girl had said—that if you didn't go to church (we never did), your body burned in hell. A body, anyway, I thought, could never burn in this snow. But then later, I'd hear the snickering voice in my head again, and when it spoke, it was almost with a sneer. Still later, I grew to know this voice well. It got stuck on things, like those beetles with hooks on their legs, and wouldn't let them go. For a short while it was burnt bodies, then other things.

But maybe, I thought, there was a way out. I pictured, as I lay in bed at night, meeting God in the garden and trying to explain. It was above all for my mother that I would plead. But would he be kind? I thought he would be sad, but also kind. I imagined as I lay there that I heard him downstairs, his footsteps and the rustling of his clothes. I should have met him in the garden! Instead I fell asleep. Now it was too late. He'd moved into the house. He was kind and sad and suffering, too—he didn't like to do this. Still, I had to save my mother, block the bedroom door. My heart was beating hard, but I wasn't quite awake. When I did wake at last, I thought I'd wet my bed. There was sweat everywhere. But then falling asleep again, I kept in my mind the image of this kind, sad, suffering God, come to do us wrong against his will, and my heart broke for him and, as I sank further, broke again, and I forgot completely about guarding the door.

During that first month at boarding school, a check arrived one day from my grandmother. In the envelope was a card, just one line, on cream-colored paper, monogrammed at the top: "You must take

French," it said. I looked again at the check, a hundred dollars, "for monthly expenses." What would I ever do with a hundred dollars? But I went to the bursar's and cashed it all the same.

On Saturdays I'd walk down the hill into town. It was a mill town with a river running through it, long coiled ropes the color of lead. There was the river and then the rest of the town. The houses were pale, close-set. Some had high porches. Along the main street there were stores, a diner. On the outskirts, the houses were less close-set. I'd wander around looking in windows and backyards. One person was a maniac for climbing plants. In others there were children's swings. On the way back up the hill, I'd count my steps, twenty-seven, twenty-eight, twenty-nine. The numbers sounded beautiful, clear and round. And in the chapel, too, on Sundays, the words between the whispers sounded beautiful and grand. The light in the chapel was a yellowish brown. Listening to the words, I remembered thinking about God, but that seemed a long time ago. All of it, the creek, my mother's garden, even Jasper, seemed a long time ago. I looked down at my hands and wrists in my lap—again that feeling. I have nothing. My life begins here, with nothing.

Talk to someone, I think, but I can't say anything.

CHAPTER 2

THEN ONE DAY, AS I'M WALKING ACROSS THE GREEN, A GIRL comes up to me. Her uniform, like mine, is too long, and she also isn't wearing the right shoes, thin leather, lace-up, that everyone wears. Hers are dark and clunky, and mine, even worse, are suede.

"Are you new here?" she asks.

"Yes," I say.

"Me, too," she says, "I'm Roe. Come see what I've found."

She leads me toward the playing fields. I check her out cautiously, sideways, as we walk. She has a lilt in her voice. (She's from the South, I learn.) She's taller than I am, with a clear oval face tilted slightly upward, a long neck and small sloping shoulders. Her nose, very pretty, is slightly crooked at the tip (once broken, I learn also), and the skin on her cheeks is strangely illuminated.

We come to the edge of the playing fields. Right where the woods begin, there's an old graveyard, small and filled with tangled weeds. There's no fence around it. On the wooded side, a few trees have pressed up between the stones.

"Nice, isn't it?" Roe asks.

I agree. A few yards from the graveyard stands a copper beech tree, its leaves purple-green and smooth roots exposed. Roe sits down, back and shoulders against its trunk. She has begun on the way to tell me a bit about her life. Her mother died when she was young. She was raised by her father, a military man.

"And he's like that," she says. She makes a chopping motion with her hand. "Very strict. Even about little things, like fingernails. You're always supposed to keep your fingernails clean." She puts out a hand and looks at hers. There's a small rim of dirt under each one. She laughs. "But I was the girl. I could get away with things."

"You have brothers?"

"One. He's older, very different from me." She leans nearer. "He's a born-again Christian."

"You're kidding."

"No," she says, "and his wife is, too."

"He's married?"

She nods. "Can you believe it? He's twenty-one. That's the marrying age in my town."

I look at her. Everything about her seems more and more intriguing. "Where's your town?" I ask.

"In Georgia," she says. She looks down at her fingernails again, begins to try to clean them. "We moved around a lot when I was little because of the military, but for years now we've lived there." She looks up suddenly. "What about you?" she asks. "What's your father like?"

"Oh—" I say, stumbling. I was so interested in her life, I'd forgotten about mine. "He doesn't, I mean—I never knew my father."

"He died?" she asks bluntly.

"No," I say. "At least not that I know of." I look at her warily. "But he left before I was born. I think my mother told him to. They weren't married or anything."

"So you never even met him?".

I shake my head. I feel uneasy.

She looks out at the playing fields. "Wow," she says, "that must be strange. My mother died when I was small, but I have a sense of her. I remember certain scenes, and even just the way it felt sitting with her."

"How did she die?"

"An accident. She was hit by a car." The thought of it is a shock. I look at Roe in awe. Already in my mind, she had assumed a certain stature, but now with this new knowledge, she seems to grow larger. She's playing with some blades of grass with her fingers. "I was always the girl in town with no mother." She smiles, looking up. "I think it gave me a certain prestige."

I laugh, surprised, then hesitate and decide, however cautiously, to go ahead. "I did have someone who was like a father, though," I say.

She looks at me curiously. "What do you mean?"

"Jasper," I say. "At first he was my mother's boyfriend, though he was ten years younger than her. But I hardly remember that, I was so small. When it didn't work out, he stayed on, setting up his house in the barn."

"He was your mother's *boyfriend*?"

"Well, yes," I say, smiling, confused. "Why, didn't your father have girlfriends?"

"No," Roe says abruptly.

"He didn't? Not once after your mother died?"

"No," she says, more slowly this time, "at least I don't think so." She pauses, looking out. "One thing's for sure. He'd die if I ever knew." She turns to me again. "So you mean your mother had other boyfriends, too?"

I nod. "Quite a few. But I spent almost all my time with Jasper anyway."

Roe crinkles her forehead, trying to understand. "And your mother didn't mind him just living in the barn?"

"No," I say. I can't believe she's actually interested. But she seems to be. I go on. "I think she even liked it. He paid a small rent, and did jobs around the house, like going into the woods and cutting down firewood or chasing the hunters away, and he took care of me." I tell Roe about how Jasper used to tell me stories. He'd go around delivering firewood to people in the area and come back with stories each time, about the three brothers who lived together on the other side of the mountain and all looked like Baryshnikov, or the crazy woman Bella, who had two little girls and was always in trouble with the law.

In the distance, as I'm talking, Roe and I hear voices, and then a group of five or so girls appears, running down the slope onto the playing fields. They have hockey sticks. I glance nervously at Roe. Will their presence break the spell? Roe's looking at them, too, but vaguely. Then she turns, shifting her back toward the playing fields, lifting her legs and hugging her knees.

"It sounds like you grew up in the wilderness," she says.

"Well, yes," I say, "I think that was the idea. My mother was raised in a very different way. Or at least that's what I always heard. When she was little, she spent almost all her time indoors with nurses. So when she grew up, she was determined to live in the countryside. Mostly, I think, to get away from her mother and that whole lifestyle."

"What lifestyle?" Roe asks.

"Oh," I say, "you should see my grandmother!"

I was coming in from the creek one summer afternoon when I saw in the driveway a long silver car. The seats inside were shiny, and there were black initials on each door. There was a man on the porch. Here to see my mother, I thought, but he didn't behave the way the others did. When he saw me, he looked down.

"Marcel!" a woman's voice called from inside the house. Behind the screen door, there was a glimmer of white. Then it opened just enough to reveal a hand. The hand glinted, it held a drink.

Marcel took the drink. "The girl's here," he murmured through the screen.

The shimmer of white paused, looked. "Well, what are you waiting for?" the same voice boomed. "Tell her to come in!"

The woman inside was beautiful, I thought, and her clothes were beautiful. She wore white pants and a shirt with a Chinese front. She had a thick waist, long legs. Her face was somewhat wolflike, the cheeks and throat powdered; her hair was dark and springy, curling up at the ends like the rim of a hat, and she wore a very strong perfume. ("Your grandmother's dream," my mother once said, "was to walk into a crowded room and hear everyone gasp.") Beside her, on the counter, were a small ice bucket, three bottles, and a stirrer, none of which belonged to our house, and at her feet was a small white muscular dog with a flattened face. The dog growled softly when we came in.

"Marcel," the woman said, "take Louis outside." She lit a cigarette and turned, studying me for what seemed like a long time.

"Do you shake hands?" she asked at last. I tried to move forward but couldn't. My hands were clammy. My shorts were dirty and torn from the creek. I covered myself with my wet towel, but it was no use. My feet remained stuck to the floor.

That night, for dinner, I put on the fanciest clothes I had. But my mother was upset, I could tell. When I came downstairs, she was tearing lettuce at the sink, her back toward my grandmother.

"Where's Marcel?" she asked quietly.

Marcel, my grandmother's driver, was still outside. He didn't seem to want to eat with us. My mother insisted he did. This made my grandmother laugh. When she laughed, she flung out one hand that flapped down loose over her wrist, like you do to brush away a mosquito or swat at flies.

"And Louis?" she asked. "What about Louis? I don't think the girl likes him. Marcel! Come in here, and bring Louis."

Marcel came inside, followed by Louis. By the kitchen light, Louis looked different, strangely bald all over, and he appeared to be shivering. He didn't growl now but stood stiff-legged, staring, seeming suddenly more stuffed than real.

"What I'd like to know," my grandmother said, "is where are all the men? When I was a young widow, my house was full of men. Wasn't it, Marcel?"

Marcel nodded. He stood gingerly by the table, refusing to sit. But when my grandmother handed him another drink just like hers, he took it, and each time she got up while we were eating to refill hers, she refilled his without asking.

"I'm not a widow," my mother said, still at the sink.

My grandmother didn't answer her. Instead she turned to me. "I've buried three husbands," she said.

I was nervous. I tried to smile. "Where?" I asked.

My grandmother was clearly pleased. She stood up again and lit a fresh cigarette. When she spoke, she had a drawl. She held her eyelids low. "Oh, here and there," she said, "around the house. I put one by the swimming pool. Roger. If you come visit, I'll show you."

I watched my grandmother as much as I could while she wasn't looking. As the evening passed, she had more of a drawl, her eyelids hung lower, and I thought she looked even more beautiful. Most of all, I longed to say something else that would please her. I felt sure I could say something wonderful if only I were given enough time to think. Throughout dinner, I racked my brain for something to say.

At one point my mother left the room. My grandmother turned, as if she could no longer contain herself, speaking half to Marcel, half to me. "It's really preposterous, this—whatever it is, hippieness, spending all day growing vegetables, doing other people's chores. If only she'd allow me—but she cut herself off. You realize that, don't you? Your mother cut herself off." She suddenly looked directly at me. "I saw a young man earlier going in and out of the barn. Who was that?"

"Jasper."

"What's he doing here?"

"He lives here."

"With you?"

"No, in the barn."

"In the barn?" She laughed. "Lovely, he lives in the barn. Is he your mother's boyfriend?"

"No," I answered. But I'd thought of something I could say. I had to do it quickly while my mother was still gone. I looked carefully toward the door, then got up and went over to my grandmother. But once there, I couldn't get the words out.

[15]

"Well?" she asked, taking a drag on her cigarette.

"She *does* have boyfriends," I whispered finally in her ear. I heard my mother's footsteps returning, and suddenly felt ashamed. "Don't tell her I told you," I added quickly and went back to my chair.

My grandmother leaned back. She smiled. "Well, that *is* interesting," she said.

"What?" my mother asked, entering the room. She looked confused, even childlike.

"Nothing." My grandmother looked at me languidly. "I promised I wouldn't breathe a word."

I felt both guilty and full of joy. Once in bed, I couldn't sleep, trying to think up other wonderful things I could say. I pictured all the wonderful things, not in words but in colors. They would be her colors, the white of her pants and throat, the gold of her many rings, the purple of one of them, a large cut stone, and her eyes, too, almost purple.

But when I woke in the morning, my grandmother was still sleeping. When I got home from school, she was gone. For days the whole house smelled of perfume. Then only the room she'd slept in smelled. Each day it smelled fainter, finally not at all.

Roe listens, her eyes shining. "There's no one like that in my family," she says.

"It's because of her that I'm here," I say. "She's paying for me to go to this school. What about you?"

"Oh," Roe says, looking down, "we could never pay. I have a scholarship." She flushes for a moment, then regains her poise and, looking almost defiant, stands. She walks over to the gravestones and peers down. "So now I'm here," she says, "and it's fine and everything.

I mean, I'm glad to be here." She looks up. "What I'm wondering, I guess, is when your life assumes its course. It must at some point."

"Yes, it must," I agree. I stand up cautiously, too.

"And then you must feel very different."

"Very different, yes." I hesitate, then say it. "Like a person."

Roe turns. "Exactly! Like a person! But what does that mean?"

I look at her, surprised. "I don't know."

"Me, neither." She smiles, eyes lit, as if to say that this is half a joke but also very serious. "Let's think," she says. "What makes a person a person?"

She walks back and forth, hands clasped behind her back, gazing at the ground. I watch her, intrigued. I walk over to look at the gravestones. On some, the lettering has all but faded away. Instead, where it should be, there's lichen in patches, shaped like tiny lettuce leaves.

"Do you know Madame Loup?" I ask.

Roe looks up. "Yes," she says. "I'm not in her class, but I know who you mean."

"She seems to me very much a person," I say.

Roe nods. "Yes," she says, "I agree, but why?"

"There's the way she walks." I try to do it, wrists and ankles loose, wobbly, on heels.

Roe laughs. "I've seen that."

"But also how she dresses. She almost always wears brown."

"Yes, she has a style." Again in Roe's eyes, there's that glimmer, half laughing. "What else?"

"The way she laughs"—I bare my teeth—"and her handwriting . . ."

[17]

"Hmm," Roe says. "But that's the question. Doesn't everyone have all these things? I guess what I'm wondering is if there's such a thing as one person more distinct than the rest." She stops, eyes wide. "And," she goes on, "if the whole aim in life is to become as distinctly yourself as you can?" She turns to me, face illuminated. But then, as I watch, the light fades. She falters, as if irritated. "But could that really be the goal? Then what about the other things, happiness, for instance?" She looks at me directly. "Is happiness your goal?"

I hesitate. "Maybe," I say, "but I'm not sure." I'm thinking very carefully. At first, when you're thinking, you just feel a hard nudge, the brunt of an obstacle. Then, if you're lucky, the obstacle goes, and there's a sudden cool flooding of the brain. "What I feel more than anything is scared," I say. "And I guess what I would like is to not feel scared."

"Really?" Roe asks. We're both standing still, facing each other over the grass. "But what are you scared of?"

I laugh. "Everything!" I'm laughing at the pleasure of simply saying it. Then I stop. "No, not everything. In fact, all I'm really scared of are people."

"Hmm," Roe says, thinking, her forehead flickering. "I'm trying to figure out if I'm scared, too. I think I am." She sits down against the trunk of the beech tree. "But I think what I'm scared of is that something will happen. Something terrible, an accident or a tragedy of some kind."

She's silent for a moment. I sit down not far from her.

"But," she says, "the truth is, it's not only that. It's actually more like I'm sure it'll happen, and I'm just waiting. I'm not only scared but expecting it, resigned!"

She turns to me eagerly. I feel a sort of thrill and a plunging darkness. It's as if we've come to the edge of something, but instead of stopping, have just gone on. When I speak again, it's through that thrilling darkness, and my voice comes out rough and hoarse. "I'm more afraid that I'll *do* something terrible."

Roe's look seizes me, quick and triumphant. "Really?" she says. "How interesting."

She drops her chin into the crook of her knees and stares out, in silence, at the playing fields. After a moment or two, she lifts her head. "No," she says, "I was trying to imagine if that's what I feel, too, but it's not. What scares me most is the world outside."

On the way back to my room that night, everything looks different. Even the light. The dusk has a shimmer. Once there, I try to imagine Roe in her room, and when I can't, I try to imagine her in general, how she looks and moves, her voice and expressions. But I can't. She's a blur in my mind, like a rush of light. Lying in bed, I think of other things that I might tell her, about running from the hunters and the snickering voice, about how everything about me feels horribly wrong. Has she ever felt that, too? Does she ever hear a snickering voice?

I feel, for a moment, as if the world has begun all over again. Or rather, more exactly, as if I've stepped into another world—shimmering, dark—where everything I've ever thought of or imagined or dreamed has suddenly transformed itself into something spoken, that could be spoken, if I dare.

ROE AND I HAVE PLANNED TO MEET AGAIN THE NEXT DAY AT the graveyard. I'm worried all morning that she won't be there, or that if she is, it won't be the same. She is there, waiting, legs stretched out and crossed, reading a book under the beech tree.

"What's your book?" She shows me, *The Idiot,* by Dostoevsky. "Is it good?" I ask.

Roe nods. She smiles and stands. Yesterday it was still. Now there's a fluttering breeze. Roe shivers and pulls her sweater tighter around her shoulders. "Should we walk a little? I'm cold."

We walk along the edge of the playing fields, skirting the line of trees.

"What kind of books do you read?" she asks.

At first I draw a blank. No one's ever asked me this. Or rather, like someone stumbling over herself, I have too much to answer, but none of it's clear. In my mind it's all a jumble, characters and settings and scenes, mixed together and tumbling forth from all the books I've ever read, in the library, on the school bus, or sitting out in the yard at home.

"*Jane Eyre,*" I say tentatively, "is one of my favorite books."

Roe's eyes light. She's read it, too. And then, as we go on, book by book falls out clear.

Roe loves Russian novels, she says. Later, lying down in the warm grass, the breeze above us, we talk about *Anna Karenina,* the only one I've read.

"Were you surprised when she did it?" Roe asks. "Threw herself in front of the train?"

"Yes," I say, "weren't you?"

Roe doesn't answer. She's on her back now, looking up at the sky. "Are you afraid to die?"

These changes of hers, these blunt questions, startle me. But I like them. "No, not really," I say. A plane flies high above us, noiselessly. It glints, traces a strip of white. "If I die, I die," I say. "It's other things that are scary."

Roe laughs. "I agree."

I glance over. I can see her profile through the stalks of grass. She seems to be smiling, but I can't be sure. A few blades waver with her breath.

"Have you had sex yet?" I ask.

"Yes." She says it matter-of-factly.

"Really?" I hadn't expected this. I sit up, flushing. "How was it?"

Roe rolls over to her side, propping herself on an elbow. "Not what I expected, but nice. We snuck away from my father. That was maybe the biggest thrill, sneaking away. Didn't you ever want to?"

I laugh nervously. "One day, yes, I do." I pause. "I did make out once with the neighbor boy, but"—I make a face—"it wasn't nice."

"Why?" Roe asks, laughing.

"I just don't think he knew how to do it. I had spit all over my face." I lie back again and stare up at the leaves. "People always seem to act like that's how life begins, by having sex."

"It isn't," Roe says, "believe me."

The thought is a relief. "Well, how then?"

Roe looks at me, her eyes bright. "I don't know," she says. "But isn't that what we mean to find out?"

ROE AND I MEET AGAIN IN THE GRAVEYARD THE NEXT DAY AND the next. I show her the bench by the chapel and take her to look at the pond. We spend hours in each other's rooms. We eat together, study together, and in the middle, stop. Lying back on either her bed or mine, we talk about our bodies:

"I wish my calves were fuller, like yours."

"But yours are nice. At least they're shapely."

"But that's just it! I feel like they have no shape!"

"I used to wish when I was little that I had curly black hair, that kind of blue-black."

"I know what you mean. I used to wish I didn't have a nose."

"Really?"

"Yes. I thought it would look much nicer."

On other days we worry that we don't have a core.

But what is a core? A dense thing inside that's always the same. Like a soul, then? Well, yes, but what is a soul? I never understood that. Is your soul like mine? Are all souls the same? Could you recognize one?

The light slants farther. September ends. The leaves begin to change. The copper beech turns a shimmering copper gold. I no longer lie alone in my dormitory room. I no longer have time. When I'm not in class or studying, I'm either coming from seeing Roe or on my way to see her. And the other girls? I no longer hear their clamor in the halls.

Roe also admits to being intimidated by the other girls, especially when she first arrived. She, too, feels sometimes when she steps out that her face is so ugly and shapeless, she wants to cover it with her hands.

"And then," Roe says, "I have my accent. And I'm poor." She says this last part offhandedly, or tries to, but at the same time flushes.

[22]

"No one would ever know," I say. "I wouldn't."

"Yes, they know," she says, "these people know."

It's not as though we don't still admire the other girls, and even envy them, we do. But they're like a spectacle we're watching. We only want to spend time among ourselves.

"Who's that?" Roe asks when we're in my room one day. There's a photograph of Jasper on my bureau. It's the one photograph I have out.

"Jasper," I say.

"You're kidding." Roe picks up the photo, peers closer. "He's so young! How old is he now?"

"Thirty-two," I say.

"And your mother?"

"She's forty-two."

"*And* good-looking."

"Do you think so?" I ask. Jasper's fair, his blond hair pulled back in a ponytail. I'd never really thought about whether he was good-looking or not.

Roe puts the photo back, looks at it sitting there. "Do you miss him?"

I shrug. "In a way, yes," I say. "We write letters. He writes me a letter almost every week." There's already a stack of them on my desk. "But in another way, it's funny, I almost have to force myself to think of him, as if that whole world no longer exists." "Do you miss things?" I ask her.

"My friend Laura sometimes," Roe says. (She has told me about Laura, her childhood friend. "You'll meet her. She's a freak, you'll see," Roe told me, obviously proud, "there's no one like her in my town.") "But I don't miss my father," Roe goes on, "at least not yet.

Maybe that's because I have to call him every Sunday"—she rolls her eyes—"I promised I would."

Another day, after classes, we're sitting in Roe's room.

"People have habits," Roe says, "and preferences."

"Yes, I know, but what are ours?"

Roe and I walk down the hill into town. We go to the diner and order black coffee. We agree that *Jane Eyre* is better than *Wuthering Heights* and that Mr. Ryan is the most handsome teacher at school. We hate umbrellas and lined paper, much prefer felt tips to ballpoint pens. We like a shoe with a solid heel. When we're old, we plan to carry canes. We look forward to being old because we imagine that by then we'll have given up worrying about anything and can just sit back together, legs up, in the sun. On the other hand, we have a great fear of becoming housewives. We swear that we'll never learn to cook or iron or sew, and can't understand anyone who likes to cook or iron or sew. We hardly brush our hair. We don't like brushed hair. Although we both have hair down to our shoulders, we plan to cut it very short very soon. And we plan to stop biting our nails one day, not now, and to read a great many things. When we begin to list the books and writers we want to read, our brains end up swimming. We imagine how it will be when we travel together, the two of us sitting side by side on foreign trains. Out the train windows, the world rushes by, flat or rocky, pale or blue or green.

The colors we like are blue, green, black, brown, occasionally dark purple. We don't like yellow or red. On the wall of her room, Roe has two reproductions of paintings of women in tropical settings, their skirts and dresses seeming part of the leaves. Roe says she'd like to live somewhere tropical. I say I might, though I'd miss the snow.

We say these things, but at the same time we can't at all imagine that we'll ever live anywhere or own things, a house, a yard, or a car, or behave in any way like other people do. When we walk through town and see people coming in or out of houses, they seem to us like foreigners, almost another species. But there's something else, too.

"I just feel like we're waiting."

"Me, too. But for what?"

For the future? For ourselves?

Roe and I intoxicate each other with our thoughts. We try to describe things to each other, feelings and situations, that seem to us so complicated and subtle, we had never imagined they could be described. Roe tells about sitting in the yard one night late and hearing her father come out and swear at the flowers.

"Sometimes I hear a voice in my head," I say. "A snickering voice. It says all kinds of things. It waits until it hits on something that really scares me, and then it says that thing over and over again."

"Why, though?"

"I don't know. I don't know what it wants. But I feel sometimes like it's trying to destroy me."

Another time I tell about running from the hunters. When the hunters came onto the land around our house, although they weren't allowed there, Jasper would go out after them. He'd be chopping firewood out behind the house, would hear a shot, and throw down the ax. My mother said to be careful, the hunters were often drunk, and all, of course, had guns, but this didn't seem to worry Jasper. Once he found a half-dead deer by the road, shot but badly, and he tried to save her, put her in the back of his car and brought her home, but by the time he arrived, she was dead.

One night as I was running down the mountain where I'd stayed again late, the dark air cool around my face and legs, a spotlight in front of me suddenly went on. I froze, blinded. I heard laughter, voices. Then I could see dimly a small group of figures, a truck parked sideways out on the road. I ran to one side, out of the spotlight. More laughter. The spotlight followed me. I ran the other way, back and forth and back again, dodging through the trees, but the spotlight kept tracking me until finally I turned around and ran as fast as I could back the way I'd come, over the hill and down the other side, all the way to the neighbor's house, where I banged and banged on the door. I was shaking, my skin ice-cold, when they brought me in. But I didn't want to tell them what had happened, and later, when my mother and Jasper came to get me, I wouldn't tell them, either. When we got back home, my mother put me to bed, but I couldn't stop shivering, and even after she'd warmed the blankets by the fire, I was still shivering, and for the first time ever, I saw that she was afraid.

Roe listens. "My father has a gun," she says.

"He does?" I ask. "Does he hunt with it?"

"No," she says, "he just has it. He has it around the house."

"Does he ever use it?"

She glances sideways. "Not that I know of. I mean, in the military, yes, I'm sure he killed people. And he'd kill someone now, too, I'm sure of it, if he felt he should."

Roe and I are both sixteen. I'm a few months older, but Roe, it seems, has seen much more of the world, while I've seen just one place very closely, and in this way, and others, we are not at all the same.

Roe listens to music; I don't. She has a flickering interest in Heathcliff; I don't. I have a crush on Mr. Rochester and an irrepressible fascination with Madame Loup.

Roe owns rubber riding boots that reach up to the knee. She has an army coat torn at the seams. Both she found in thrift shops in her Georgia town. When she isn't wearing her uniform, Roe wears men's clothes, pants and coats and shoes, either bought at thrift shops or taken from her father's closet at home. Since arriving at school, I no longer know what I wear.

"Show me what you have," Roe says. She opens my closet and looks at my things. "The key, of course, is to come up with your own style. This, for example"—she pulls out my cloth raincoat with a patterned lining—"or this," a gray sweater with black stripes at the cuffs.

Roe likes water, I like woods. She spent years by the shore. She loves the sound of waves. I can hardly imagine what waves sound like. What I hear instead are wood sounds, the sounds of plants and small animals and trees. I'm very fond of plants and trees, but Roe is afraid of sprouting things. Her nightmares are often about things sprouting, reaching out white roots and gripping on to things.

I almost never remember my dreams. Roe remembers hers. She narrates them to me with a hallucinatory precision, so they often seem more real than the day we're in.

For the mandatory sport, I take soccer, Roe ballet.

Once, after sports, as we were walking in across the grass instead of on a nearby path, a teacher with iron-gray hair whose name we didn't know came blustering after us.

"What is this? Who are you? There's a perfectly decent path, yet you insist on destroying the grass!"

"Excuse us, sir," Roe said, "we were absorbed in conversation." Her voice had a much more pronounced southern twang than it usually did, and I realized, to my surprise, that she was playacting.

Roe was schooled as a child in the rituals of politeness—this, too, her father was strict about—but she's also not opposed to playacting, pretending to be someone she's not. It seems to me that I don't know how to playact and just grow paralyzed instead, like that day when I ran into Mr. Ryan by the pond.

"You did?" Roe asks.

"Yes. This was before I met you."

"What happened?"

I tell her. I was kneeling down looking in the water—filled with algae, a murky green—when I saw him approaching, head bent, along the path. He didn't see me. I froze, then, out of nervousness, stood abruptly. He jumped, afraid. He was by now very near.

"Oh, hello," he said. "Sorry I scared you."

"No—" I said.

"Yes, that's right. It was the other way around. You scared me." He smiled, distracted, and went on.

Roe wants to learn Russian. She also wants to be a photographer. She has a small plastic camera that a teacher at her school gave her years ago. She has a shoe box of black-and-white photographs that she gets out one day to show me. They're of places or people in her town, a tree dripping moss, a dog lying outside a building, a row of children squinting at the sun. "The beginning," she says, "of my brilliant career."

I tell her about how I used to keep a notebook where I wrote down the stories Jasper had told me, and then, after a while, I began to make up my own.

"Is that what you want to do, write?"

"Yes," I say. I've thought it before but never said it aloud.

We picture how she'll be in five years or so, by the Black Sea with her camera, recording Russian scenes, and how I'll be, writing in Paris and wearing brown.

The diner, as we talk, fills and empties around us. There are two waitresses. One is soft-limbed and cheerful; the other, wiry, is always rolling her eyes. But at this hour, they both behave the same. Languid and bored, they sprawl across the counter, staring out, waiting for the end of the day. When we're not talking, Roe and I stare out, too. We always try to get a booth by the window so we can watch the street. Mostly we see the daily life of the town, the policewoman putting tickets on people's cars, kids playing in the abandoned lot farther down. They whack at weeds with sticks or try to climb the fence. One day we see a furtive girl from school, older than Roe and me, sneaking a cigarette in the shadow of a corner building. Each time someone passes, she puts the cigarette behind her back, afraid that if it's a teacher she'll be caught.

Roe and I love it when it starts to rain. Softly at first, the street gets speckled, then harder, the street is dark and dancing with drops. Roe and I ask for the check. The sky darkens; storefronts blur. We get our coats. The sky cracks. We step out. There's a roar above, and then the rain comes hurtling down.

Outside, a curtain of rain falls before our eyes. The houses seen through it seem to be leaning downhill. We follow them. Rain pours over us as we walk. It pours over our faces and into our mouths. It runs down our legs and into our shoes. Our feet get soaked. Our hair grows heavy and darkens. Our clothes darken and droop. We keep walking, we don't care! The street widens at the bottom of town. There's a shopping center and then the river beyond. We head toward the river. The rain is thick. We can hardly see in front of us. If we want to talk, we have to scream. We can hardly see each other, but what we do see makes us laugh, a thick-haired, huddled screaming thing, a witch or a banshee. What if someone sees us? Let them see us, we don't care—if we ruin our uniforms, destroy our shoes, catch a fever and are put in the infirmary, get horribly sick there and die. We've agreed that we're not afraid to die, though we are, as we've established, afraid of something.

The rain grows softer. We come to the river. It's dull gray, as always, but now thrillingly swift. Standing on the bridge and looking down, Roe shivers. She hears, she says, a snickering voice, too. "Only it's not alone. There are two voices battling. There's a voice that fights against the snickering one."

"Really?" I ask. "It tells it to be quiet?"

"Well, yes," Roe says. She lifts her hand and unsticks the hair from her face. "Or at least it talks back."

"And," I persist, "which one of them wins?"

Roe looks down at the river again. She pauses, considers. "I think it just depends."

On the other side of the bridge run train tracks edging town. Sometimes Roe and I go sit under the wooden awning and wait for a train to come by. Occasionally there's a woman there, in her forties, going to see her sister's family, as she once explained to us. She carries a yellow purse and is usually bringing food, a cake or a stew in a tall pot. One day there was a young man standing outside the awning, along the tracks, in the sun. The sun hit the gravel and the rails and his hair, sleek and dark. Slender, with an insolent look, he smoked cigarette after cigarette. We watched him from inside the awning, peering through the cracks between the boards. He had delicate shadows under his eyes. Over one shoulder, he carried a small leather bag.

"Let's ask him for a cigarette."

"I dare you."

"You do?"

Roe got up suddenly and left the awning. I watched her uneasily through the boards. Purposeful at first, she then faltered, flushed. The young man was looking the other way. Roe cleared her throat. He turned, surprised. She got her high southern voice. He stared at her. It was as if he were pinning her with his black eyes. Suddenly I felt not just nervous but afraid. Did he think she was alone? His hair and eyes glinted like the rails. I felt a blur in my head, then I saw it all clearly, him gripping Roe by the neck, her mouth open, hair flying, behind them the jolting clamor of the train. I jumped up and rushed out of the awning. They both looked at me, startled. They were silent. The tracks were empty. Roe's head was bent, a cigarette to her lips. The young man, a pace away, had his arm out toward her. He flicked a lighter casually, once and then again, while Roe, hair falling forward, bent near and inhaled.

"Thanks," Roe said, rising, but her voice was constricted. She tried to smile and coughed instead, a stutter at first—smoke shot from her nose and mouth—and then a heavy wild cough that made her double over. The young man grinned. Roe flushed deeply and turned away. Still bent over, she came toward me. Her face was dark, and the veins in her neck bulged against the skin. I followed her back into the awning, where we both sat down.

"Are you all right?" I asked.

She nodded. She was coughing less vigorously, but she still couldn't speak. She handed the burning cigarette to me. I took it and sucked in. After several seconds I felt it, too, a hitch in my throat. The hitch grew tighter. I fell forward, neck out, and coughed.

"Shhhh!" Roe said.

The young man was still outside. I tried to cough silently, gripping the bench. But it wasn't just the cough. I felt dizzy. I felt like sinking down onto the ground. I passed the cigarette back to Roe. Roe cleared her throat and inhaled again. Her lips looked very thin and pale, as if under a great strain. Her eyes and the rims around them were red. I had never seen her looking so sick.

"Here," she whispered.

She handed me the cigarette again. She was still holding her smoke in. I took another puff and held it in, too. We both sat silently, pale and not breathing. Then Roe convulsed. Not just coughing this time. It sounded wheezier, like I imagine a seizure might sound. I thought she might be choking but then realized she was just laughing, not her normal laugh, which was watery and high-pitched, but a strangled, smoke-filled laugh. I began to laugh, too. Then I stopped. I grabbed my throat. It was so sore, it felt as if the skin had been removed.

Just then the woman with the yellow purse arrived, but instead of saying hello as she usually did, she glanced at us disapprovingly and walked on past, stationing herself a few paces outside the awning. For the next few minutes, she stood there stiffly, casting quick, furtive glances over her shoulder at us and then the young man, who was himself smoking again, until Roe, between laughing and coughing and trying to suppress both, couldn't bear it anymore and got up and ran out of the awning, the half-smoked cigarette held out behind her back at me—"Take it! Take it!"—while I, also collapsing, followed, and together we made our straggling way back to the bridge.

But today, instead of stopping by the train tracks, Roe and I walk on, up along the river past diminutive houses perched on muddy lawns. Some look as if they might tumble into the river, while others are pristine, their shutters blue or cherry red. We pass a young boy standing in rubber boots and staring out expectantly at the rising river. A car pulls up to the house. He runs back inside. The rain has stopped. A pale, slanted sun is slowly coming through.

"Jane Eyre has her self-respect. She keeps saying that. But what does she mean?"

"It's not pride."

"No, definitely not pride. It's something much more solid."

"Do other people have it?"

"Do we?"

Roe's army coat is dry at the shoulders, but the hem still drips. We turn down an alley and circle back toward the center of town. From the alley we see the backs of things, hedges, fences, houses, cars. There are garages and garbage cans. Everything is still wet. Things are darker, but they glisten. The pavement in the alley is cracked. It bulges up and breaks. Grass grows in the grooves.

On the main street, we turn again. The wiry waitress from the diner is getting into her car. It's powder blue. She's still in her waitress uniform. She rolls her eyes at us, at how wet we are.

We head up the hill, stopping first by the drugstore, for pens and chewing gum, and then by the thrift store, a woman's house, really, with a sign outside, to see if there's anything new. The house is broad, with gabled windows. Above the mailbox is a bell on a string. We ring and wait. After a moment the woman lets us in. Inside, the high front room is packed with things, furniture, lamps, jewelry, dishes, and glassware, racks of dark clothes, a row of old shoes. The woman, suspicious at first, knows us now. She's already sold us two full-body long-john suits, a peacock feather, a lamp, a pair of men's shoes. In her sixties, she, like Roe, is a curious dresser. She'll be wearing, for example, feathered mules when we arrive, or some funny combination, a turtleneck with an angora sweater vest. She has a full-cheeked impish face and eyes whose expression is half-adventurous, half-scared.

Roe throws an expert glance across the room. She's been shopping in thrift shops her whole life and is an old hand.

"Here," the woman says, watching her, "this is new."

She holds it up, a gold lamé bag. Roe shakes her head and smiles. The woman smiles. She puts the bag back down on a pile of others, then, one hand still clutching it, peers vaguely around the room. She's a mystery to us. She never seems to leave her house. So how does she accumulate all these things?

We wait. After a few seconds, she drifts out into the room, touching here the neck of a lamp, there a low cane chair. It's a ritual each time. She shows us what's new. Roe and I look at what she shows us, then look on our own. Roe flips through the rack of men's pants. I'm never exactly sure what to do. I open the drawers of various pieces of furniture. In one I find a clump of old hair. I shut it without saying anything, then look up at the owner. It's not hers.

She hovers by the window. The blind behind her is pulled, but it's

[34]

a thin white blind, letting in a filtered light. Her hands are folded but lifted, up near her stomach, poised there, waiting. Her eyes are almost exclusively on Roe. Roe almost always buys at least one thing. Today it's an ivory comb.

Outside, the sun is low and gold. Walking up the hill, the wind blows our hair flat across our faces, then, as we turn a corner, swoops it up and back.

"I just feel like my face is blank," I say.

"Don't worry," Roe says, "I recognize you."

"You do?"

"Yes."

"Even when I'm not with you? If you just see me walking?"

"Well, yes, you have your walk."

CHAPTER 3

IT MUST BE AROUND THIS TIME THAT I FIND THE DRESS.
I don't remember exactly, only that one day after classes, Roe and I pass
by the thrift shop again. It's mid-October. It's been raining again and
has grown chillier. Bright, wet leaves plaster the ground. The woman
doesn't come when we ring the bell. We wait, and as we're turning to
leave, we hear her, muffled, fumbling with the door. She's wearing a
flowered robe. But it's not this that's strange. It's her face. She has
makeup on, sky blue eye shadow and pale pink lipstick, smudged up
her cheek to one side. Under the robe she wears a black negligee.

"It's chilly," she says once we're inside. She looks at what we're
wearing, Roe her army coat over her uniform, me my cloth raincoat.
"Maybe you need overcoats?" she says.

"Yes," Roe says vaguely, looking around.

The woman steps toward a rack of overcoats at the far end of the
room. Roe and I follow, but on the way there, something catches my
eye, a sliver of pale green between the rows of dark clothes. I reach
for it, touch it. It's a dress, hideous on the one hand, when I take it
down.

Roe turns. "Did you find something?" she asks.

I hesitate, embarrassed, then show her the dress. It has small sleeves and a high waist. Roe looks at it, surprised. For a moment I think she's going to laugh. But she doesn't.

"Hold it up in front of you," she says. I do. She tilts her head, looking. She's not convinced but doesn't dismiss it, either. "The only way you'll know is if you try it on."

"Yes," the woman says. She steps over to a curtain hanging in one corner and pulls it aside.

I take the dress behind the curtain, where it's dark, and put it on. Even in the dark I can tell it fits. But it's not just that. When I step out again, Roe sees it, too. Her face lights.

"Come," she says, and has me turn around. The skirt billows slightly, then falls back to my knees.

"Yes," the woman murmurs, stepping up beside Roe, "it suits her. I never would have thought it, but it does."

That's the word. It *suits* me. It is like, and Roe and the woman see it, too, an unlikely but unquestionable solution to a predicament.

"What about your hair?" Roe asks.

"Up, no?" the woman says. She finds a barrette and pins and puts my hair up on my head.

"There," Roe says when it's done. I turn. Suddenly, in the mirror, I'm an indeterminate age, very young or much older. The woman takes a silver lipstick holder out of the pocket of her robe. She dabs a bit of pale pink lipstick, the one she's wearing, on my lower lip.

"Just rub them together slightly." She demonstrates, then watches me do it.

"Now shoes," Roe says.

We look together down the row of shoes, high heels, boots, low heels, mules, sandals, slippers, clogs. Roe hands me some boots with buttons up the side and then a pair of white sandals with square heels. But it doesn't matter. We all know it, the woman, too. The dress is enough, and the hair. Everything else suits or no longer matters. I've already stepped out, passed through.

"But you mustn't wear it now," the woman says quickly. I've paid for the dress, but I still have it on. "It's cold."

"Oh, but I have to," I say, surprising myself.

On school days, no matter where you are, you're supposed to wear your uniform. But my raincoat is long enough to hide the dress. Walking up the hill with Roe, my uniform bunched in my bag, in the silver-green dress no one can see, I try to imagine how I must have looked earlier walking down. Different, I feel sure. Not at all like this.

Something happens, and you forget to be afraid. When I was little, I used to picture that Paradise garden. I'd read about it in a book at school. Once you step in it, you're no longer afraid. Wolves gather at your feet, flowers dip down at you, a snake drinks water out of your hand.

By now we've cut across the road and are heading toward Roe's dormitory under the trees. "You know what I was thinking?" Roe asks after a pause. "You say you feel scared, but I think what I really feel is numb. Not on the surface, exactly, but underneath. Like a dead person, almost."

She smiles as she says this, but I know she's also serious.

"Really?" I say. I'm trying to grasp it, the outer living layer—which seems so alive, flickering and mobile—and then the dead part. "You would never know that from looking at you."

"No? You wouldn't?" Roe asks, pulling open the front door of her dormitory. As in mine, there's a narrow flight of stairs immediately afterward.

"No," I say, struggling to express it, following her up the stairs, "and especially, I mean, because you seem so interested in things."

"I am, though, I am," Roe says. "What I'm talking about is different, much further in." She walks down the hall. "As if there's something like a limb asleep, only it's deep inside me and can't be moved."

We go into her room. There are clothes on the floor; the bed is half made. On her desk sits a lamp from the thrift shop. A peacock feather stands propped against the windowsill. Roe sits down at the chair by her desk. Out the window in front of her is a gold tree. She's looking down absorbedly.

"What I want right now is to feel alive, the whole way through," she says. "Or at least woken up."

She looks at me. The gold shimmers on her face.

ROE DISCOVERS FROM A GIRL IN HER DORM THAT WE CAN GO into New York City on weekends if we get a day pass. She tells me over dinner in the dining hall. "A bus picks you up at the top of the hill."

"And you go? Just like that?" I went to New York once with my mother when I was small, but otherwise I have no experience of the city.

"Well, yes," Roe says. She's spent time in cities before. Her family lived in Austin. "But you have to be back before curfew. Unless you get an overnight pass. You can also do that. Someone in the city has to write a note and invite you. Or at least to *say* they're inviting you."

"What do you mean?"

"This girl in my dorm says she sometimes has her sister write, pretending to be her aunt."

I already feel something in my stomach. It flutters and lifts. "Well, let's go," I say nervously. We agree to get day passes for the following Saturday.

On Saturday Roe picks me up at my dorm. I'm wearing the green dress, over it a raincoat. She, as usual, wears a button-down shirt and pants. We walk over to the top of the hill where the bus stops, the sky above us clear and blue. There's a cluster of girls already waiting. We notice what they're wearing—on the weekends we can wear our own clothes—and who they're with. But we don't feel any need to associate with them. While waiting for the bus, we stand to one side. Are we outcasts? When a smooth older girl gives us a cool look, we're convinced that we are. On the other hand, we feel somewhat superior. No one, we think, talks about the things we do, or has discovered the things we have. No one, we think, is quite so interesting.

When the bus comes, Roe and I sit together in the back. This is not a school bus but a real bus, from the world, on its way into the city. I look around. The seats are high-backed. There's a rack above them. Beside us is a woman reading, her face tipped forward. She has dark, carefully shaped eyebrows, a middle part, very white, almost searing against the black of her hair. Farther up, across the aisle, I can see only the bottom part of a leg—it must be a man's—a heavy foot, rumpled pants.

The bus moves off. I feel jittery already. Roe slouches beside me on the seat. "Do you think we could pass?" she asks softly, eyes glinting. "For people, I mean, and not just students?"

We're sheltered from the other students by the seat in front of us. I look at her, her illuminated cheeks, slightly crooked nose, collared shirt like a man's.

"I think you could," I say.

"Really?" she asks, pleased. She looks at me, tilts her head. "Turn away," she says. "Pretend you don't know me." I look the other way, out the window. The golden fields are flashing by.

"Yes," Roe says after a moment. "You look very particular. Not at all like a student."

"Really?" I say. "But I feel all jittery. Can you tell?"

"No, not at all. The opposite, in fact. You look very deadpan."

We exchange more compliments, then fall silent. I drum my fingers on the glass. The fields rush by in gold or brown squares. The leaves ripple on the trees, red and gold and green.

NEW YORK CITY. NO MATTER HOW GRADUAL THE APPROACH— the reds and golds turning to purples and grays, the puffs of trees replaced by lines of buildings, the grass growing sparser, then more taller buildings with more and more windows, wedged together, mismatched, cars, fences, streets, everything wedged right in—still you're not ready for it. How could you be? Emerging from the tunnel, suddenly you're there. The stone everywhere, the concrete rising outside the bus windows, as we lurch and veer and turn. And the airiness, I hadn't expected it. Stone and air. The broad avenues with islands in the middle planted with small trees, cars on both sides sweeping by. Then more stone, more sweeping air. The roominess, there's room for everything on the wide streets, for everyone, buildings high, there's even room for the wind. It seizes an avenue, whips down it, hair is blown up, coats, shirttails, newspaper sheets and trash. A building on the corner shivers, entirely in glass.

Roe has told the bus driver that we want to get off on the Upper West Side. We're looking for something, a thrift shop. Roe has the name written out on a card. Her friend, Laura, from her town told her about it. It's the only precise place we know of in the city, the only lead we have.

Riverside and Eighty-sixth Street. Roe and I step down from the bus. We walk one block over to Broadway. Once there, we don't know which way to turn. We're at a corner. There's a trash can, a newspaper stand, a row of public phones. A smell of crushed fruit mixes with the smell of fumes and things being fried. A line of cars surges forward. Roe and I step back. Up on the sidewalk, a man in a cowboy hat and a red cowboy shirt sweeps a few strokes with a broom, then holds out a cup for change. A woman behind him shouts in Spanish into a telephone. We sway one way, then the other. We bump into each other. Roe grips my arm, though not looking at me, her face dazed, gazing out.

Then, as if on impulse, she steps forward. I follow. The sky is very blue, the light clear on the buildings. I look at Roe walking beside me, her lope, her small shoulders and illuminated cheeks. She's familiar, but it's not just that. She's wearing her shoes. She walks like herself. Like a person, I think. She looks like a person. And if she does, I think, maybe I do, too. Besides, we have a task. We're looking for this thrift shop.

Walking down Broadway, we pass a bag lady sitting on a stoop. She has layers upon layers of different-colored clothes on, including, beneath everything, a flowered summer dress. A young black man leaning against the brick wall of a supermarket holds out his hand. "Give me five," he says. Roe hesitates for a split second, then does as we walk on by. A man in a business suit stands outside a bar singing love songs at the top of his lungs. He holds a briefcase. He's drunk, wears a well-made suit. This must be what he's wanted to do his whole life, sing love songs in public at the top of his lungs. Two young women in fabulous oufits on fabulous block heels walk by. "Sing to me, honey," one says to the man. The other, giggling, clutches the first one's arm.

It's that suddenly intoxicating feeling. The gap between action and desire narrows and, at certain moments, simply falls away.

The thrift shop is on Seventy-seventh Street at Central Park West. We get to Seventy-seventh. On the corner is a newsstand, newspapers and magazines, candy, cigarettes and cigars.

"Excuse me, sir," Roe asks, with her high southern inflection, "we're looking for Central Park West."

The man is in his fifties, grizzled, friendly. He points. "Three long blocks that way."

"Thank you, sir," Roe says. "Oh, and a pack of cigarettes." She turns to me. "Camels?"

I nod, playing along.

We take the cigarettes and a pack of matches and walk away. Halfway down the block, we step into a doorway out of the wind and, huddling there, light a cigarette. We take a puff each. But we're huddling there, hiding. I look out down the street, then at Roe. I laugh. "What are we doing?" I say.

I step out of the doorway onto the sidewalk, the cigarette in my hand. I take a puff in full view of everyone. Roe steps out, too. She takes a puff and blows it out, coughing only slightly at the end. We walk along, passing the cigarette back and forth, until we arrive at Central Park West.

Across the street is the park, the low stone wall, the trees behind. Turning, we see, a few doors from the corner, a purple sign, Go Ask Alice, and black metal stairs leading down.

The door at the bottom of the stairs opens to the sound of a bell. Inside, a woman stands behind a counter talking on the telephone. She barely looks up as we step into the room. I'm still looking around, but Roe, within seconds, has seized it all clearly.

"This is like my dream," she breathes.

There are racks and racks of not only clothes but hats, wigs, shoes, boxes of jewelry, a basket of gloves. The room seems to go on and on. All along the walls are mirrors in gilt frames. And then more racks, more boxes and trunks of things. Mannequins stand poised at strategic points, modeling here a suede jacket, there a sequined dress.

Then, behind us, there's a noise. The door to one of the dressing rooms opens, and a boy steps out. He's slim, about our age, with an extraordinary face, bony but very smooth, and he's wearing a woman's dress with a garish turquoise pattern. It fits him slimly. His hair is cropped roughly, and he wears black lace-up boots. Roe and I look at him, amazed. When he sees us standing there, a flush slowly creeps up his neck and face. He hesitates, as if he might turn back into the dressing room, but steps forward instead. He goes toward a mirror and looks at himself. I pretend to look away but can't help watching him. In the glass I can see him watching us, too, carefully, quickly, as he looks at himself. He's still flushed but, it seems now, also exhilarated. He wants us to see him. Then he goes even further, stepping over to the row of mannequins and lifting off one of the wigs, long and curly, blue-black. The curls cluster around his pale face, then fall like tendrils down to the arch of his long slim back.

"Isn't that the hair you always wanted?" Roe whispers.

I smile and nod, but I can't take my eyes off the boy. Neither of us can, though we try to behave as if we're looking at other things. Now, with the wig on, there's no clear sign that he isn't a woman, or a girl like us. His expression is amazed, too, and pleased. He takes one last look and turns, walking back past us to the dressing room.

Once he's out of sight, Roe turns to me. Her face looks excited, suffused. She surveys the room. Her eyes light on a rack of men's collared shirts. I look for dresses. I'm thinking of the boy. Where did he get his? Then I see them, a whole gleaming row, short and floor-length, hanging there, waiting.

Roe is collecting shirts. She, too, like the boy, has a wig on. I've found a gold dress with a belt. The boy comes out of the dressing room a moment later, wearing pants and a shirt. His pants are so loose that he has to hold them up with one hand. He looks at us shyly, but also with intent. We don't say anything. Roe smiles slightly. He walks up to the cash register, the dress over his arm, the wig in one hand.

By the time Roe and I leave the thrift shop, also with purchases—I get the gold dress, Roe two shirts and a wig—an hour or so has passed. We buy sandwiches at a deli and, eating them, drift into the park.

The park paths are lined with people and their dogs. The shadows of the trees are lengthening slowly between the bright patches of grass. Here and there are piles of fallen leaves. In the middle of the park, we come upon a glittering green lake with a path around it. We stop for a moment to watch a toy sailboat race, the small white triangles turning and turning, kids and parents cheering on the shore, then walk on along the path, past a group of ducks and old men on benches, two of them leaning over a chessboard.

Farther on, the path dips down. It's dimmer, the undergrowth thicker. We come to a stone tunnel, an underpass—above it runs a road—with thick, shiny vines climbing up its sides. On one side of the underpass is a door to a public bathroom and beside it a drinking fountain, flooded, the cement at its feet wet and dark. There's no one around. Roe and I look at each other and giggle. We have an eerie feeling. Then we bolt through the pass. It's pitch black and damp inside. Our feet make a crashing sound. When we come out on the other side, it's fresher but still dim. We're low down, the leaves on the trees thick here, so much so that the streetlights are on, shedding a thin brittle glow over the path up. We climb the path until we see the lake again, its dull patches and glistening pods. Ducks swim separately. A jogger passes. Then it is very still.

We hear his footsteps first. I turn. It's a young man with a greasy face and choppy bangs. He's close behind us, his hands in his pockets, gripped there. Then he swerves over and starts walking beside Roe.

"Hey," he says, hands still deep in his pockets. He dips his head forward to nod at me. "What are you girls doing?"

Roe answers in her drawl, "Nothing much."

I can't believe she's answered. The boy has taken his hands out of his pockets and is twisting them in front of him as he walks. There's no one around. I look at his hands. My heart starts beating faster. He could do anything to us, I think. "Come on," I say softly to Roe.

I speed up. Although I don't look at her directly, I can see her beside me in profile, walking as quickly as I am. Up ahead, I see a fork in the path. We'll turn there, I think. But the boy has sped up, too.

"What's the rush?" he asks, walking beside Roe. Roe doesn't answer, but she's listening. I can feel her listening. The boy has focused completely on her. "I have something to show you," he says.

Roe glances over. She actually looks, I catch her. By now we've come to the fork in the path. I veer to one side, taking Roe's arm. She comes, but is she reluctant? I can hardly believe it. She turns with me, but there's a faint dragging pressure of her weight on my arm.

"Hey, where are you going?" the boy asks. He's stopped at the fork. His eyes are on Roe.

Roe hesitates for an instant, but I can feel her there suspended, not going toward him but not turning away, either. Then she does move, I feel it. The weight of her body, illuminated, shifts toward him.

"Roe!" I say. "Roe!" My whole being is fixed, vibrating, with terror.

Just then a man appears, coming toward us along the path. He's tall, and pushing a wheelchair that holds a tiny Asian woman in a padded purple coat. Roe snaps and turns. She comes back toward me. A wind lifts suddenly, deepening the ripples on the lake, making the leaves all chatter. I feel the relief run through me, down my limbs, like water. My body feels like water, as if I may collapse. I see a bench and want to sit down but don't. There are more people around us, the paths no longer deserted. But it still feels dangerous.

"Let's go," I say. "Let's keep moving."

Roe walks beside me in agreement, almost docilely. But nothing about her movement seems particularly scared. Instead, her eyes glow. I look over at her. I feel like shaking her by the shoulders or turning my back on her, but I can't because we're walking.

"What were you doing?" I finally ask. I can taste it in my mouth, almost like disgust.

"What do you mean?" Roe asks.

"Then! Just then! You were going toward him."

"No, I wasn't," Roe says.

"Yes, you were. You were!" I'm furious.

Roe is embarrassed. She doesn't answer but walks on quietly.

"I was curious," she says after a little while, softly but clearly.

We walk on in silence. The reflections of the leaves fall over everything, the paths and the benches and the wavering grass.

ROE AND I GO INTO THE CITY THE FOLLOWING SATURDAY, TOO. We return to Go Ask Alice and then eat lunch in a Dominican diner we find on Broadway, La Rosita, it's called. There are small Formica tables, a counter like an arm bent at the elbow. Instead of potatoes, they serve you rice and beans or fried plantains with your eggs. Afterward, we buy cigarettes and head toward the park. This time, on our way there, I suggest stopping somewhere to buy a six-pack of beer.

"Really?" Roe asks. "Do you think we even can?"

First we look for a liquor store. Then we realize, to our relief, that delis sell beer. We find one and walk in together, but then Roe goes back outside. She stands there watching sidelong through the window as I buy the beer. The man at the counter eyes me as I'm paying but doesn't say anything. I sweep out a moment later in triumph, carrying a large brown paper bag.

"Now where should we go?" Roe asks.

"To the park," I say. I'm picturing those large rocks and the underbrush and that very black shade. "But let's get an opener."

We stop at a hardware store to buy an opener and then continue on to the park. It's just past midday. The sky is white with layers of clouds. There's a chill. In the park the leaves are gold, half fallen. We take a turn and come upon a row of cherry trees, confused by last week's warmth, blooming out of season, their small pink flowers looking strange and bright against the gold of the leaves.

We walk around inside the park for a while, lugging the paper bag. We take turns carrying it. It's not especially heavy, but it's awkward to carry—there's nothing to hold on to. We're looking for a place to sit down and drink our beer, but nowhere seems to be quite right. We pass a policeman. Is this illegal? We're not even sure or not sure what part of it might be. Then I see a group of rocks high above the path, surrounded by underbrush. I climb up to look, but just as I'm motioning for Roe to follow, I hear noises to my left. I turn. There's someone in the bushes, a figure wrapped in blankets. The figure moves, rolling toward me. I clamber back down through the rocks to Roe.

"No," I say, "forget it. There's someone there."

Roe leans back on her heels. She puts the bag down on the ground. She seems to be losing interest. I pick up the bag and lead the way. The light is dull, the park nearly empty. We walk on.

Finally I find a spot that seems to be right, some bushes up against a stone wall. I duck down to look. There's no one there. I crawl in. Roe follows. The branches on the bushes arc upward, then fall. They have small oval leaves. If we sit with our backs against the stone wall, the branches fall in front of us, making a screen. But they're transparent enough that we can still look out and watch people passing. Beneath us are brown fallen leaves, dried out. They make a crashing sound when we sit.

I take the beer out of the bag. The bottles are bright green. I open two and hand one to Roe. She takes a sip and makes a face. "It's disgusting," she says.

I smile. I take a sip and wince, too. The beer is cold and we're cold, too, now, our noses and fingers red. Roe puts her bottle down on the ground and rubs her hands together to warm them. I take a longer sip. The wall, rough at first against my back, feels softer. "You have to take a longer sip," I tell Roe.

Roe lifts the bottle to her lips, puts her head back, and holds it there. I can see her throat pulsing as the beer goes down.

"Like that?" she asks, giggling, as she brings her head down. Her bottle is nearly empty. Then: "Whoa," she says, reeling, after a moment. She puts her arms out to steady herself, although she's firmly sitting on the ground. She looks at me. "Do you feel it, too?" she asks.

I nod. Cold before, I now feel warm. But it's not only that. My mind feels different. It's as if something in my mind has come unclutched. My thoughts, jagged before, now feel smooth. Nothing disrupts them or jerks them back. They flow along smoothly and all seem to be related, harmonious even, whereas before they weren't.

Roe and I have almost finished our beers. I open another two. As I'm drinking my second one, I try to explain to Roe what I mean about my thoughts flowing smoothly and easily.

"It's as if they all joined in one stream flowing through my head," I say, "as if before, they weren't flowing but jabbing sideways, arguing, yes arguing and gnawing at me, and suddenly they've stopped and are just flowing along together, wishing me well."

"Have you ever gotten drunk before?" Roe asks.

I nod. I tell her about the time I got drunk with Jasper. I must have been around thirteen or so. My mother had gone out for the night with her boyfriend. I was at Jasper's. He was drinking a beer, and I took a sip. Then I asked for one.

He let me have it. Almost immediately, I felt different. It was starting to grow dark outside, I remember. Jasper's face looked unfamiliar in the blue light, but not in a bad way. Everything, I thought, looked friendly and soft. I felt happy and warm, no longer frightened. Or it was as if I realized only then, when I was no longer frightened, how much of the time I actually spent afraid. The feeling was so different, I started laughing. Then I couldn't stop and collapsed in a giggle attack on the floor.

"Oh, boy," Jasper said. "What's got into you?" He came and stood over me. "I wish you could see the way your hair looks right now," he said. It was spread around my head like a fan. "You know, we could probably fix it up that way."

We went into the bathroom where the mirror was. He started teasing my hair up. Pretty soon it stuck high in the air all around my head.

"There," he said, "you look just like Bella now." Bella was the woman he told stories about. She always wore her hair like that, high around her head, her clothes dipping off the shoulder to one side.

Jasper had another beer, and I did, too. He put the music on and we started dancing, me with my hair high around my head. I had a sweater on, I remember, and I kept letting it fall down off one shoulder like Bella did.

When my mother came back late and found us still dancing and drinking, her expression was peculiar. I couldn't place it. Both Jasper and I were bleary-eyed.

Roe smiles as she listens, her head lolled back. She seems to be enjoying this, or so I think, until she abruptly jerks her head up, makes a sharp guttural sound, and throws up on the ground. She stumbles up, hitting her head on the branches, then ducks again, putting her hands in front of her to shield her eyes, and crawls out almost frantically into the air. I follow.

I find her outside on the path, wiping her mouth with the back of her hand.

"Are you all right?" I ask.

She shakes her head and wipes her mouth again. She says she wants to get the early bus back to school.

We walk together to the edge of the park, wait without speaking for the bus to come. Roe doesn't feel well, but I feel fine. In fact, I feel like humming. Roe sits down on a bench, but I trail along the park wall, stepping and humming.

I come upon the bag lady we saw before on Broadway. Now she's sitting up on a ledge that juts out from the park wall. I walk past her. Her feet are up. She wears that same dress covered with hand-sized pink and purple flowers, and on top of it, various sweaters and coats. She has sandals on her feet and thick socks. The socks under her sandals are filthy. She could be any age, it doesn't matter. Her face is puckered flesh.

She doesn't seem to notice me as I pass. She has her bags all around her, everything she needs. She doesn't have to lift a hand. And she doesn't. Except sometimes to drink from a paper bag. Or to put a sweater on or take it off. Otherwise she sits there surrounded by her things and watches the people passing and the stream of cars. The only things that rile her are the pigeons, when they come and settle on her bags. Then she flaps her hands and beats her bags in a fury, but soon sinks down again, forgets and goes on watching. One pigeon, as if to tease her, remains. She doesn't notice or else doesn't care anymore. Petlike, it stays.

I make my way back along the wall. Passing her again, I think, I wouldn't mind that for a life.

When the bus comes, she suddenly rouses herself. "Good-bye!" she shouts, waving. "Good-bye! Good-bye!" I turn and wave back as I'm climbing the stairs.

On the bus Roe looks at me, almost with reproach. Then, a moment later, she falls asleep, her head lolling on the seat. But no matter what I do, I can't seem to shake my good mood. I sing very softly at the window, my breath fogging the cool glass. Everything outside looks wavy and strange, as if we're underwater, the roads and clouds, leaves and fields. Sitting there looking out, it seems to me that I feel for a moment utterly happy.

But Roe doesn't. When we get back to school, I wake her up. She still doesn't feel well, seems almost angry.

"Let's not talk to anyone," she says and walks away, heading toward her dormitory.

"Are you all right?" I call after her.

She wobbles her hand without looking back at me, almost dismissing me. For some reason, her wobbling hand makes me laugh.

I turn the other way and follow the thread of my song, trailing it like a leafy vine down the paths, along walls, around corners and curves, all the way back to my room.

JASPER CALLS. HE SOUNDS ANXIOUS.

"Why haven't you answered my last letters?" he asks.

I don't know what to say. I don't know myself. I tell him I've been busy with schoolwork.

He has news. He's moved out of the barn.

"Really?" I ask. "Why?" Suddenly I feel concerned. "Where are you living now?"

"Oh, I rented a little place, half a small house, not so far away."

I picture him all alone in a rented house. I have a wild thought: I should go live with him. Of course I should. What was I thinking, going away to school?

"But listen," he says, "I want to come see you."

"Oh." I hesitate briefly, then lie. I tell him that they don't allow visitors at school.

I hang up quickly, quickly get my coat, and go to meet Roe.

In the hours before curfew, when the other girls are studying or watching movies in the auditorium or having huddled secret parties in their rooms, Roe and I go out and walk in the night. We walk past the dormitories and the faculty houses and out across the playing fields. The graveyard is bathed in damp cool forest air. The copper beech is rustling above.

"Don't you really want to meet someone?" Roe asks, leaning against the beech tree's trunk.

"Yes, I think so." But I sound hesitant.

"You're not sure?"

I kick at the leaves around our feet. "I guess I'm just wondering if we really want to meet someone, or if we just feel like we're *supposed* to?"

Roe looks at me. "Do you think that's all it is? We just think we're *supposed* to? Because everyone else does?"

I shrug. "Well, what's the other possibility? It's instinctual?"

"Maybe," Roe says. We start walking again along the edge of the playing fields. "There's Laura, for instance. She sounded so happy in her letter." Laura has written Roe recently to say she's discovered she's gay. She met someone, a woman; that's how she found out. "Now, she wasn't *supposed* to do *that,*" Roe says. "Her mother's completely scandalized."

We walk on without speaking. We've circled around and are climbing the slope that leads to the Green.

"Of course, no matter what," I say, "it's sure to be an experience."

"Yes," Roe agrees, "and isn't that what we want?"

"No matter what it's like?" I ask, making a face.

"I think so," Roe says.

I look up. The Green stretches before us, the small dark shape of the chapel at its end. We head toward it.

"So the question," I say, "is how to meet someone."

"And of course we don't mean just anyone, right?" Roe adds. "We mean *the* person."

I picture the way Jane Eyre meets Mr. Rochester, on the road one evening, and the way Catherine and Heathcliff have known each other their whole lives. I mention this to Roe.

"But is there anyone you would even consider who you've known your whole life?" she asks.

"No," I say. The only person I've known that long is Jasper.

"Me, neither. So we'll both have to meet someone."

I agree. "Do we wait for him to come along?"

"This waiting!" Roe says. "Waiting again!"

We sit down on the stone bench along the chapel wall. Before us are the black outlines of trees, heavy pines. All around us wind.

Suddenly it occurs to me that it might not be that easy, might not even happen at all. "What if we never find the person?" I ask.

"Or what if, when we do, he doesn't want us?"

I laugh. "Wouldn't that be awful? And then what—we'd end up alone?"

Roe shrugs. "I don't know," she says. "We're sitting here together, aren't we?"

"Yes," I say, "for now. But what about when life starts?"

I can see the outline of Roe's face in the darkness. "Hasn't it started?" she asks.

She says it as though it's obvious, but I'm surprised. "Do you feel like it's started?"

"Well, yes," Roe answers, "I sort of do."

At other times we fall silent. The night air is cool. The wind blows through the trees.

"What will happen?" we ask each other after a little while. "I mean, what do you think will happen now?"

CHAPTER 4

THERE ARE VARIOUS PEOPLE WHO COME TO OUR DOMINICAN diner in the city: a couple with a dog that waits for them outside; an old woman with what must surely be her daughter, a slightly younger version of her. Among them one day is a man. Watching him idly, I point him out to Roe. Though I couldn't say exactly why, everything about him appeals to me, the way he holds his shoulders and leans back in his chair, legs stretched out. And then the way he catches himself, leans forward abruptly, impatient, goes back to what he was reading or writing. His eyes, dark like his hair, are set deep. For a moment his expression is even morose. When he leaves, he leaps up all at once as if he can't bear to sit for another second.

"How old do you think he is?" I ask Roe.

She shrugs. "Thirty? Forty?"

The truth is, we have no idea. Though he is, we decide, definitely a man. The transformation has occurred in his bones and skin, in the way he moves, in his expression, in the way, on leaving, he has a brief friendly talk with the manager, as if he's been doing this for years.

The following week, when we arrive, this same man is there with a friend. He's agile, animated, as he talks. He lifts his eyebrows, moves his hands. Or, when he's listening, he relaxes completely, his hands lying loosely in his lap. The friend leaves. Our man goes back to his papers and books. Half an hour later, someone else appears, an older man who could be his father, Roe and I decide. The older man's coloring is pale, his features somewhat finer, but the lips and eyes, the general bearing, are the same. They order food. Throughout the meal, our man looks uncomfortable, even irritated. He folds and unfolds his hands, pays for the meal. The older man, his father, seems lighthearted, shifty, somewhat flittish. His pale watery eyes wander out to the street, then back to his son and the meal at hand. The father leaves first. The son slips him money on the way out, then remains behind with a discontented look.

Although Roe and I still watch and comment on the other people in the diner, this man becomes the focus of our interest, or at least of mine. He's here, I think, when we arrive, or he's not. Another day he's with a woman. She wears a blue coat, has a small, pretty face. She furrows her brow. Seemingly disturbed at first, their conversation grows warmer. Her back is straight. She speaks softly, her face glows. It almost seems from the expression on his face that he loves her.

Then they begin talking about something else. The conversation turns. She grows insistent, leans nearer. She's upset. He tries to remain amused. Then his eyes flash. But his anger is ironic, contained. She stiffens with reproach. I watch all this with a growing uneasiness, and interest, too. What could they be fighting over? How did they get to know each other so well? The fight ends, finally. On his face there's a look of fatigue, but the anger's gone. He looks not old but affected by life. She, too, looks ruffled, exhausted. But her face is also drained of its previous nervousness. They're both calm. They grasp hands. The table is wide between them.

"Don't stare like that," Roe says.

"Am I staring?"

"Yes."

But she's been watching, too.

"Do you think that's his girlfriend?" I ask.

Roe shakes her head. "No," she says, "not now. Maybe once, though. There *is* something strong between them."

Roe and I have talked about the man we'll one day meet, the man who will one day recognize us. (That's what we want, we've decided, to be "recognized.") Will he be short or tall? Dark or blond? I have a figure in my mind, but I can't fix it, it keeps changing. Sometimes the man I see is Mr. Rochester from *Jane Eyre,* sometimes he's at least partly Mr. Ryan. Now this man from the diner gets mixed in with the rest. Sometimes, quite simply, his is the face. I picture the way he can grow morose, and wonder if, like Mr. Rochester, he has a terrible secret. I wait for the day he'll recognize me.

One day he looks up while I'm watching him. His eyes seem to catch mine. But is he really seeing me, or just staring out, absorbed in his own thoughts? In any case, I can't hold his gaze, and look away. When I look back, his head is bowed, reading again. Was that it? I wonder. Was he recognizing me? And now that I've turned, he thinks he's made a mistake. I feel desperate for a moment—I've lost my chance.

But unexpectedly, half an hour later, I get a second one. Roe and I are leaving the diner—he left a short while ago—only to find him standing outside on the curb. He's reading a newspaper, not paying attention. He must be crossing the street. We are, too, on our way to the park. I feel nervous at the thought that we'll be crossing with him.

He's already stepped out from the curb. Then I see it, a bus coming, heading straight toward him, barreling fast. He's not paying attention, not stepping back. The bus is nearer and nearer, bearing down. In an instant, without thinking, I jump forward, throwing my whole weight against him sideways, body checking him back to the curb.

He looks up, startled. He's knocked off balance, reaches out to steady himself on the hood of a car. The bus is passing right in front of us, the breath and clamor of it less than a foot away. Then it's gone. He turns to me. The street is clear. He looks shaken. I feel shaken, too.

"Did you do that?" he asks.

It occurs to me that he might be angry. I nod, afraid. I also can't believe what I've done.

"It seems impossible," he says. I notice a trace of an accent in his voice. He looks at me, then over at Roe, then back at me. "You nearly knocked me down."

I redden, thinking I've made the whole thing up. The bus wouldn't really have hit him at all.

"But you saved me." He laughs. "I think you really did." He looks shaken, but also amazed.

"I did?" I ask. My voice sounds small. But I feel incredibly relieved.

"I'm Arthur," he says. He holds out his hand. We both shake it and say our names. "Could I offer you something, a coffee, to thank you?"

I'm nervous. "We just had one," I say. Oh, no, I think, what have

I done? "But we're going to the park," I add quickly, "do you want to come?"

He looks at me, surprised. "You're going to the park?" he asks. I nod.

"And you're inviting me to come?" He's trying to get not so much the facts clear as the reason behind them.

I nod again. Is it a ridiculous suggestion? Is he making fun of me? I flush and look down.

He looks at his watch, then back up at me, puzzled and amused. "I have a meeting in twenty minutes," he says. "But it's in that direction." He tips his head toward the park. "I'll walk with you until then."

It's a bright blue November day, the sun clear on the buildings, the air bracing. Roe and I are silent. We walk a pace or so ahead, almost ignoring him. He tries to keep step with us, amused.

"That really was remarkable," he says to me. "The way you jumped out, you nearly killed yourself."

I shake my head without looking at him. Now that he's agreed to join us, I have nothing to say.

"Do you two always walk so fast?" he asks.

I drop the pace abruptly. Roe does, too. Now we're creeping along, barely moving. The man looks as if he might really laugh.

"Well, we needn't exaggerate," he says.

"What?" I ask.

He says it again. Besides the accent, the turn of phrase is funny. When I understand it, I jolt forward again, trying to walk faster. But my legs won't move normally. I feel them locking. They lurch forward strangely. I'm certain he'll see this.

The park is just a few blocks away. I continue to say nothing, Roe likewise. The man seems to be enjoying this more and more. "I feel as if I might be being led to the slaughter," he says.

Roe giggles. I'm embarrassed, but then I feel almost angry at the way he's making fun of us.

"Well, why are you coming, then?" I ask.

He stops walking abruptly. He laughs outright. His face opens clearly when he laughs. "Because you invited me," he says, lifting his arms. "Besides which, you just saved my life."

But he *has* stopped walking. Does that mean he won't come now? Roe and I have stopped walking, too.

"Do you not want to come now?" I ask.

This makes him laugh harder. "Yes, I do, I do!" he says. "If only because this is one of the most peculiar invitations I've ever received."

We all start walking again. He looks over at us, raises his eyebrows. There's no trace at all of his morose look. He even seems to be making an effort to keep himself from laughing.

We enter the park. Out of nervousness, and since I still haven't come up with anything to say, I pretend to be interested in observing the surroundings, the trees and dogs, the patches of grass, as if I've never been here before.

But I can feel Roe on my other side, preparing something. Finally she blurts it out. "Are you American?"

The man accepts her question gladly. "Thank you for asking," he says. "Yes and no. I'm half. You're wondering why I talk like a beast?"

"No—"

"Of course you are. That could be the only reason. My father's

American, and my mother's Romanian, but it's not her fault. I grew up in France. I've been here for many years, but I still can't seem to talk like a human being."

Roe giggles. I forget for a moment about trying to walk normally.

He goes on, behaving very cautiously, with a sort of mock caution. "And do you two live here in New York?"

"No," I say, "we go to boarding school."

"Ah!" He claps his hands as if everything, for some reason, has come suddenly clear. "Where is your school?"

We tell him the name of our little town.

"Yes, I know it," he says. He seems delighted by this news, as if it has revealed something about us, though without spoiling the image he had in his mind.

Again I feel somewhat defensive, as if our situation is ridiculous in a way we don't know. "What's so funny?" I ask.

"Nothing. Nothing's funny. It's just that it makes sense. So you're marooned out there with nothing to do."

We've come to a bend in the path. We turn. The lake opens before us. Frozen before, it's thawing in the sun. Clumps of ice float on the bright water. Roe and I head for the bench we always sit on.

"And are there boys at your school, at least?" the man, Arthur, asks.

"No," we say.

"No? But there must be a boys' school nearby?"

"Yes," we say. We shrug. We sit down on the bench.

He laughs. He sits, too. "So nothing impresses you," he says.

"That's right." He leans back, hands behind his head, looking up as if remembering. "You two are at the age when nothing impresses you."

Again, for some reason, I feel ruffled. "I don't think that's true," I say.

"What?" he asks, surprised.

"That nothing impresses us. I think things impress us."

"You do?"

Roe nods, agreeing.

"Like what?" he asks.

"Like everything, anything." I say it as if it's obvious, almost as if I've been offended. "Things we read and see."

"Each other." Roe laughs.

"Yes," I say, "we impress each other."

"Maybe that's true," he says, "but in that case you don't betray it. That's the key, not to betray it."

Roe and I both light cigarettes and puff on them sitting side by side. Arthur watches this with amusement.

"Do they let you smoke at school?" he asks.

"No." We shake our heads.

He looks at us, still leaning back, his legs stretched out. "I have a sister about your age," he says. "You two make me think of her." Then he looks at his watch and turns to us squarely. "I have to go in a minute. But one question first: Do you two always go around inviting people to come with you to the park?" He pauses, but only slightly. "Because I wouldn't," he says, "I really wouldn't."

He stands. "But thank you all the same for inviting *me*." Is he just being polite? He does seem amused. Still, I feel that there's been some sort of misunderstanding. He's amused, but that's all. He was supposed to behave differently, to "recognize" me.

"You're going already?" I ask.

"Well, yes."

"Where?" I ask bluntly.

"I have a meeting."

"For work?"

"No," he says, slightly taken aback, "a personal meeting." He pauses. "But I really do want to thank you for what you did," he says to me. I try to detect if there's irony in his voice, but he seems to be speaking seriously now. He looks at both of us and goes on. "If you're ever in the city again and need anything, either of you, directions, advice, or if you ever get into any sort of trouble—not, of course, that I think you would—you can give me a call." He reaches into his pocket and pulls out a card, writes a number down on it, and hands it to me. On the card above his name is the title of an art magazine.

He puts out his hand. Roe begins to stand. I follow suit. "No, please, don't move," he says, lightly again. He shakes our hands as we're sitting there. As he's releasing mine and turning, he picks a piece of stray string off the shoulder of my coat.

"Oh, sorry," he says, eyes lit, mock ceremoniously, as if he's made a grave mistake, and puts the piece of string back exactly where it was, "I don't want to ruin the effect."

Then he's gone.

AT SCHOOL IT GROWS COLD AND SNOWS ABUNDANTLY. THE snow piles up, deep on the playing fields. Drifts form against the gravestones in the graveyard, the lower ones nothing more than mounds. The paths are shoveled clear. Now they're more like tunnels, drifts rising on each side. The snow is one thing, deep and soft. But then one night it rains and freezes. In the morning the trees all flower with ice. It's as if everything has been sheathed, wrapped over, each briar and bush, branch and twig. Everything flowers, glints, and drips. Roe and I walk out together into this new world.

The paths are laid with ice, then littered with salt. It crunches underfoot. The walking is fine along the paths but less so when we go beyond, launching ourselves out into the full snow. While before, the snow was simply deep, now it's encrusted, each step breaking through. Diverging from the path, we cut out toward the pond. There's a bare stretch of ground, then a strip of woods. The pond is just beyond, surrounded by trees.

We lift our legs high. We grow hot and tired. Roe is ahead. She enters the woods, then stops and looks back at me. I come up behind her and stop, too. Inside, it's like a fairyland, glinting and still. There's the soft white ground; above, through the net of branches, the bits of blue sky; then everything else glinting and flowering. If you look closely, you can see inside each ice casing the dark vein of a branch or the hook of a briar. But from a distance, the illusion is complete. From the highest twig to the lowest briar, it all looks as if it's made out of one thing, this same glinting substance, magical matter. Then, out of the stillness, there's a brittle sound—we turn—and a high, quick movement, ice shattering down, loosening its grip on the branch of a tree.

The pond, when we get there, looks like any other piece of dry land heaped over with mounds of snow. We can identify it only as a bare spot with a fringe of trees around its edge. But we want some surer sign that the pond is really there, the surface of ice waiting, thick and deep. First we try to step out on it and slide. The ice under our feet is smooth, but the snow on top so deep it muffles everything. The crust of the snow is hard. When we try to push through it and slide, it hurts our shins. We try to push through it and can barely move.

We decide to throw a rock out and try to break through to the water. It's my idea. There are very large rocks, boulders almost, set up as markers all along the path. But they're buried, like everything else, deep beneath the snow.

We bend down to look for one, digging through the snow. They've been placed, we know, along the shore. After a moment, digging with arms and hands, I hit on something hard. I feel all around it. Yes, it's a boulder.

"Here," I say, "I've got one."

I bend down to lift it, but can't alone. Roe trundles over and joins me, reaching down and gripping hold of the rock. Together we try to heave it up. Then we want, if we can, to fling it out onto the ice. We get it high enough in our arms, then swing it back and forth, back and forth again, then a third time, and let it fly. It doesn't go far, but it does hit the ice. We hear a deep muffled sound, then silence. A moment later, when we're no longer expecting it, there's a groan—almost human, or could it be an animal?—followed by a roar, the mass of ice shifting, breaking, then a swallowing sound. Roe looks at me, startled. The stone has fallen beneath.

We go on to the chapel. I look over at Roe as we walk. Her nose is very red, her eyes water. Her coat is half buttoned. She's not at all used to this kind of cold. The chapel bench is piled with snow. We clear it off. Ice has gathered in the corners. We sit for a moment. Ice sheaths the branches of the other trees, but on the pines it runs like water, hangs like cloth. Before us, by the chapel, the pines' swooping branches are draped with cloth.

Next we head over to the playing fields, passing my dormitory on the way. We see Mr. Ryan out in the yard, digging through the snow, as we were doing a moment ago. What could he be looking for? We crouch behind a bush and watch. He's mumbling to himself. There's his wife's face in the window. Roe giggles. The sound is muffled by the snow, but he hears something anyway and looks up. I cover her mouth with my hand. He goes on digging. Then he seems to have come upon what he was looking for. He grapples with something, lifts it. It's a tricycle, turquoise blue against the snow. He holds it up in one arm high above his head, like a barbell, victorious, shaking it toward his wife's face in the window. She laughs. Roe and I giggle quietly. We're crouched behind the bush. Roe lets herself fall back into the snow. It's thick and deep. It rises up around her. I do the same. Roe lays her head back. We're tired. We've been laughing. The snow is soft. Might we stay here forever?

But after a moment we feel the cold. Mr. Ryan has gone back inside. We lift ourselves up and go on. When we get to the playing fields, we stop. We look out. All across the playing fields are gleaming waves of snow. At the far side we see our graveyard, a higher group of huddled mounds. If only we were lighter, we think, if only we were still children, we could walk all the way across without falling in.

Back in my dorm room, we sit hunched up on the floor, our knees against the radiator. I turn to Roe. Her cheeks are bright red, her hair tangled from her hat. I hesitate, turn away, start again. I'm trying to think of a way of broaching the subject of the man we met, Arthur, of somehow bringing his name up into the clear.

"What?" she asks when I turn to her again.

"Nothing," I say. The feeling is unfamiliar, this awkwardness with Roe.

"Tell me," Roe says.

"That guy, Arthur—" I say. "Do you know who I mean?"

"Yes," she says, "the guy from the diner."

"Well," I say, taking a breath in, "have you thought about him?"

Although we talked about him on the bus ride home, his name hasn't come up again.

"No," Roe says, "not particularly. Why? Have you?"

I nod. "Yes." I bite my lip, waiting to see what she'll do.

"Really?" Roe asks, her eyes on me, questioning, trying to register this. It's a side of ourselves we haven't shared and couldn't have, not having lived it, not knowing ourselves; a kind of revelation, it's been unclear up to this point who would appeal to each of us.

I plunge forward. "Yes, and I don't know what to do."

"Well, what *would* you do?" she asks.

I shrug. "Call him."

She's still for a moment, absorbing the idea. I wait. But her answer comes faster and more lightly than I'd expected. "That's right, you have the number," she says. (It's come back to her, the card.) "Well, call him. See what happens. Why not?"

She has decided, it seems, to see this as an adventure. In this light, it seems easier. Yes, of course I should call. But she seems at the same time so blithely disengaged. I feel almost irrationally irritated for a second, as if it's somehow unfair that I'm the one being forced into this position, to call and compromise, while she, sitting there, remains fully herself.

Roe goes back to her room. Evening comes and night. I try to do my schoolwork, but I can't think at all. My mind turns all night in bed. It clutches at things so I can't quite sleep, but can't wake entirely, either, to see what they are.

The next day, all day, my mind keeps jarring. Will I call? Should I call? What will I say? The sun is strong. The ice drips and drips from the trees. If you look up, it's blinding. It all happens so quickly, some bushes and branches already entirely shorn. Call, I think, call, you have to, call now.

But I wait until the dinner hour, when the dorm empties out, the halls are quiet. The phone is out in the second-floor hall, where everyone can hear. You have to talk standing. I wait until the last girls leave. Then I creep out, the card he gave us in my hand. Heart pounding, I pick up the phone, start to dial, then stop. I look over my shoulder, listen. No one. I take a breath and start again.

I call the home number. It rings three times. A voice answers. It's his voice, a man's voice, the faint accent, a touch of impatience, but then I realize with relief that it's not really him but the answering machine. I wait, try to say something. I can't. I hang up the phone. Then, a second later, I dial again. It's busy. I hang up, wait, and try again. The same thing happens—the machine, his voice, I wait too long and hang up again.

I go quickly to my room and shut the door. I sit down on the bed tensely, on the edge, as if waiting for someone or for something to happen, then get up and pace back and forth from the desk to the door. I'm not sure what to do, where to sit or go, how to occupy my hands. I go out into the hall and try calling again. Again I hang up. I feel mortified. I go back to my room, pace, come back out, call again. I repeat this operation again and again, call, hang up, go back to my room, come back out and call again until I'm moving without thinking, each action seems senseless, yet I'm more and more agitated each time. Finally, below, I hear the front door opening and the voices of the first returning girls. I was about to call once more but instead put the phone down and go back to my room. Exhausted, I lie down on the bed. It's very dark out now, the windowpanes gleaming. I can hear the girls chattering as they come up the stairs, then laughing together out in the hall. Lying there, breathing, I come to a conclusion— I can't do this. I simply can't. I accept it with what feels like calm resignation while, with the other side of my brain, I go on planning how I'll call him again, what I'll say and what he will and how the future will be.

Another day and restless night. The water is running off the trees, their bare, wet branches dark against the snow. Everything, all that loveliness, so quickly disappeared. I'm feeling more and more shut up in my mind. My thoughts are jagged, like black bugs. They leap before my eyes, clutching and clinging.

That evening I try calling him again. It's the answering machine, and I hang up again. The next time, though, he answers. At first I'm confused. It feels more than anything like an interruption—I'd been counting on the answering machine. But then a second later, I hear it, really hear it, his voice. My face lights, my chest. "Hello? Hello?" he says. But I've waited too long, its already too late. Devastated, I hang up the phone.

I go to my room. Even more agitated, I pace around it near the walls. Somewhere along the way, I drift out into the middle and stop. It's as if a pool of water has cleared in my head, its wrinkled surface suddenly smooth. "I'll go. I'll just go," I decide.

"You spoke to him?" Roe asks when I tell her I'm going. It's the following day. We're eating lunch in the dining hall.

"No," I say. Even to her, it's a painful confession. The night before, it felt like an illumination. I can't speak to him over the phone, but in person it'll be different. I'll be different and he will. It's when I utter this aloud that it sounds somewhat questionable, even fantastic. "No," I say, "I'm just going to go."

"You'll go?" she asks. "Without telling him?" She's obviously impressed. She looks behind her, as if someone might be listening. "You'll go, just like that?" She's whispering, amazed. "And what—" she says, "what if he's not there?"

"I'll come back."

Roe looks at me, eyes wide. But her manner is still hesitant in the way mine is. It's only here, with this subject, that we balk. Then, after a moment or two, she breaks through. Her eyes glow, her cheeks. "Wow," she says, wondering. "Good for you."

Friday night I stay up late. I've already decided what I'll wear. I feel calmer now that the decision's made, almost as if from here on in, the rest is inevitable. I think of the scene in the garden between Mr. Rochester and Jane Eyre in which she confesses her love and then he does. Then I see another scene—it must be out of a Hemingway novel—I'm traveling with Arthur on a train through the mountains, I have a scarf over my hair.

The next day Roe comes with me to get the bus. She waves

as I'm climbing on. If afraid for me, she doesn't show it.

On the bus, I sit by the window and watch everything rushing by, the fields and farms and telephone poles, the wayside houses under snow. When we enter the city, I hardly recognize the streets. Snow rises on the ledges and doorways of the buildings, heaps up on street corners. Cars in snowbanks haven't stirred. It looks like an entirely different place, completely foreign, under so much snow.

I call Arthur from a public phone. I'm nervous, but at the same time I do it almost matter-of-factly, as if I have no choice. I say I'm the girl he met last week, on the street outside the diner, that we went to the park together. He interrupts, saying he remembers, he knows who I am, but he seems surprised to hear from me. I say that I'm in the city again.

"Should we meet?" I ask quickly. Otherwise I'm afraid he won't want to.

"Oh," he says, confused, "well, sure—"

"Now?" I ask.

"Is everything all right?" he asks. "Are you with your friend?"

"No," I say, "she couldn't come."

I hear his voice changing, concern in it now. "Where are you?"

I tell him I'm right near the Dominican place.

He says he already has plans, he's meeting a friend of his in the neighborhood for dinner. It's close by. Why don't I stop in and say hello? I can tell from his manner that he thinks something's wrong. I want to explain that's not it, everything's fine, only the effort's too exhausting and involves too many words. It's all I can do to agree to his suggestion and note down the address and the time.

On my way to the restaurant, I think of the bag lady in the

flowered dress, lounging in a doorway or up on the park wall. Oh, to live like her, taking on nothing, making no plans.

I find the restaurant, then circle around the block several times. Finally I force myself to go inside. Arthur and his friend are already there. It's a small place, Italian, with wooden floors. They're sitting in a corner, talking and laughing, with a bottle of wine. The friend has red-blond hair, lazy, dim eyes. He sees me first, fixes his eyes on me. Then Arthur turns. He stands, his expression both puzzled and concerned.

"I thought you might not come after all," he says. He studies my face, trying to match it with the voice he heard on the phone. "This is my friend Lionel," he says, "this is—"

"Maya," I say quickly, thinking he's forgotten.

"I know, I remember your name," he says, still concerned but now also amused. "And you said it again over the phone. I was just telling Lionel about you and your friend."

"Oh—" I say, embarrassed. I take off my coat. I'm wearing a black dress underneath, short-sleeved.

Arthur glances at it. "Won't you be cold?" he asks.

"No, I'm okay," but as I say it, I feel the goose bumps creeping up my arms.

Out the window of the restaurant, there's a high pile of snow.

"And what happened to your friend, Roe, isn't it?" Arthur asks.

"She had a term paper," I say.

"That's too bad. I was just telling Lionel about the two of you, sitting on that bench smoking away. You made such a nice pair."

Lionel's eyes are still unnervingly on me. To avoid his gaze, I look around. The tablecloths are red-and-white-checked. On the walls are autographed photos of glamorous people—Italians?—none of whom I know.

"Do you know this place?" Lionel asks.

I jump, thinking at first that he's asked me the name of one of the Italians. "No," I say. This is all a mistake, I think, I should just leave.

"Arthur says you go to boarding school," Lionel goes on. "Where are you from originally?"

My throat feels tight. "Massachusetts," I say.

"Sorry," he says, leaning nearer, "I can't hear you."

I say it again.

"You're whispering," he says with a fluttering smile.

"Massachusetts!" I say, but I must have shouted. The woman at the table beside ours turns.

"That's right," Arthur says, smiling. "Stick up for yourself."

Happily, then, the waiter appears. He's young, Italian, wears a crisp white shirt. "Are you ready to order?"

Arthur says we're having drinks for now. He asks what I'd like. I shrug. I can't think. I say I have to go to the bathroom. I spend a great deal of time in the bathroom even though there's an open grate near the ceiling sending in a cold draft. Before coming out, I make a decision. When I get back to our table, I say I have to leave.

"You do?" Arthur asks. "Really?" He tries to hide his surprise. "Well, but—are you sure you're all right? You're a little pale. Would you like something to eat?"

"Here," Lionel says, emptying his water glass and pouring me some wine. "Have a little wine. Then you can go as soon as you want."

I already have my coat on again, but I sit for a moment on the edge of my chair. I take a sip of the wine.

"Cigarette?" Arthur asks, raising his eyebrows.

I take out my cigarettes.

"Here, I'll light it for you," he says and strikes a match.

Lionel, saying he's not a smoker, takes a cigarette, too. He drops his eyes, lighting it, then lifts them again, watching me. I wish he wouldn't. I look down.

"How old are you?" he asks.

Arthur coughs. His expression is wry.

"Eighteen," I lie. I've rehearsed this, so I manage to say it.

Lionel nods, letting the smoke drift slowly out of his mouth. "So you graduate this year?"

I nod.

"And then you're a free woman?" He smiles. He seems to have forgotten about Arthur completely.

Arthur, annoyed, scrapes back his chair. He asks Lionel an entirely unrelated question about someone they both know. Lionel answers, and as if they've both fallen into an old medium, they begin to talk. After a moment Arthur turns to me to explain. They were at college together, roommates their first year. They hadn't seen each other for years, have recently met up again only by chance. They're talking about a common friend from that time. I nod, sip the wine, relieved to have them absorbed in their own affairs. I have a second cigarette right after the first. I feel my arms relax, I sit back in my chair.

When the waiter comes by again to ask if we're eating, Lionel says yes. "We're all eating, aren't we?" He smiles at me.

Arthur turns. "Only if you want to," he says, "because you're not obliged, no matter what Lionel says."

I take another sip of wine. It feels warm in my stomach. "I'd like to," I say.

The waiter hands us menus. I order the first thing I see.

The two of them go on talking as we eat. I nod here and there, ask a small question, but mostly I just watch them. Lionel, though handsome, with a high forehead, hair slightly receding, has the look of a china doll, small soft features, porcelain skin. In comparison, Arthur's features are strong. His hair is thick, his skin darker. There's irony in his expression, the way his eyes can flash. Lionel is ironic, too, but everything about him is dimmer, softer, his voice, his pale eyelashes, his eyes, semiclosed, the red-blond hair rising off his arms and hands.

I try to imagine their daily lives, what comes before and after this, their meeting in the evening in a restaurant like this. At a lull in the conversation, I decide to ask. "Do you live in apartments?"

"Yes," Arthur says. "Why? You seem suspicious."

"No—" I say. I shrug. It seems they're waiting. I'm about to feel ashamed—the truth is, I've never known anyone who lives in an apartment—and I was about to confess this, shy with shame. But then I seize on a new tack, a different way of saying exactly the same thing—"I've never known anyone who lives in an apartment"— lightly, playfully, as if it's less a failure than a discovery, even an achievement of some kind.

"Really?" Lionel asks.

"In that case," Arthur says, "you're right. It *is* suspicious, *very* suspicious."

I pursue my line of questioning. "And do you have jobs?"

"Why, yes. Yes, we do," Arthur answers.

"What do you do?" I ask.

"Oh, I'm boring, I'm a lawyer," Lionel says. "And Arthur, well, Arthur, what *do* you do? You're an art critic, right? The last time I saw you, you were writing a book, about something fantastic. Cathedrals, wasn't it? But now what—you're working at an art magazine?" He turns back to me. "So, yes, to answer your question, we have jobs. Why, are you surprised?"

Arthur's face lights slowly, understanding. His smile is tender. "We're grown-ups," he says.

Lionel laughs. "Yes, we're grown-ups. That's right. To think it could be interesting. Grown-ups! I haven't heard that word for years." Lionel seems not only amused but excited, even exalted. "Oh, to be young, to be young!"

After dinner, out on the snowy street, Lionel leaves us reluctantly. He has to go home to his wife and kids. His son, he says, is waiting up for Lionel to read *Tom Sawyer* to him aloud.

Before going, he turns to Arthur. "Whatever happened to that book you were writing? You had a contract and everything, didn't you?"

Arthur nods, smiles. "It's still there," he says.

Lionel shakes his head. "You're crazy." He turns to me. "Watch out for this crazy Romanian," he says, slapping Arthur on the back, smiling at me.

Once he's gone, Arthur and I stand alone. The street is lit up by lamps.

"He has kids?" I ask.

Arthur nods.

"And do you?"

"No, no, I don't."

"Are you married?"

"No. Listen, it's nine o'clock. Don't you need to get back to school?"

"No, it's fine," I say dismissively, waving a hand.

"What do you mean, 'it's fine'?"

"It's fine," I say. "There's a bus at eleven." I'm feeling loose and a little loopy. "Let's go get another drink."

He looks at me, raises his eyebrows. "You want another drink?"

"Yes."

He shrugs as if giving up, smiles slightly, and starts walking.

He takes me to a bar he knows in the same neighborhood, a brief walk away. The bar is on a corner. It's dark inside and narrow, with wooden booths and a pool table at the back. From a distance, the pool table looks like a little green lawn with a light hanging above it. Shadows gather around it, materializing only when they lean into the light, then retreating, then materializing again.

We sit down by a window near the front. Arthur asks what I'll have to drink. I say I have no idea and tell him to choose. I watch as he goes up to the bar. He says hello to the bartender, a rabbity-looking man with horn-rimmed glasses and his sleeves rolled up. He says hello to a dark-haired woman sitting at the bar. I imagine how he must have been doing this for years, speaking casually to people in bars.

He's brought us gin and tonics.

"Do you come here a lot?" I ask.

"No," he says, "I used to. Now I rarely go to bars."

I take a sip of my drink. I couldn't feel more comfortably settled in my seat. "This is very nice," I say, "this bar, I mean."

"I'm glad you like it," Arthur says. But he seems a bit uneasy. He looks down at his hands on the table for a moment, then back up at me.

"Your friend's nice," I say.

He nods somewhat briefly.

"Why did he call you the crazy Romanian?"

"Oh—" He looks slightly annoyed. "To annoy me, I guess." He glances away toward the pool table, then back at me.

"I don't agree with what he said about being young," I say.

Arthur looks curious. "What did he say?"

I imitate it. " 'Oh, to be young, to be young!' "

He smiles. "Why, what do you think?"

"I think it must be nice to be older."

"Why?"

"Just, I don't know, for a thousand reasons. So you can come to places like this."

He pauses, studying me. "Well, you're right," he says, "it *is* nicer to be older in some ways." I take a long sip of my drink. He sips his, too, slowly, seeming more at ease. "It sounded as though something was wrong when you called," he says. "Was there something wrong?"

"Oh," I say. I cover my mouth with my hand. "Why? Was I acting very scared?"

"No," he says, "but your voice sounded funny."

"I was acting ridiculous, wasn't I? When I got to the restaurant, I could hardly say hello."

[82]

"Nervous, let's say, not ridiculous. But don't worry. Your discomfiture was charming. People never realize that their discomfiture is charming."

I look at him. It strikes me as an entirely novel idea.

"And then," I say, "remember when I came out of the bathroom, I said I had to leave?" It all seems very funny now, and absurd. But it's as if, in my mind, the person who did that is no longer me, as if I'm remembering how someone else behaved. "Should we get another?" I ask. I've finished my drink.

He looks at my glass, impressed. His is still half full. He hesitates slightly as he stands. "You want the same thing?"

I nod. His hesitancy for some reason makes me want to laugh.

Again I watch Arthur standing at the bar. The dark-haired woman is gone. I watch his face as he waits. I remember seeing him with the man Roe and I thought might be his father. When he gets back to the table, I ask him about his family, if he ever sees them.

"I see my father when he needs money." He laughs. "Otherwise he keeps a low profile. But," he goes on, "I shouldn't complain. My brother's the one who really covers for him."

"What's your brother do?"

"He's a banker. He lives in Philadelphia."

"And your sister?"

He smiles here. "Oh, she's a schoolgirl. She's fine. Like you."

At ten-thirty, Arthur takes me to the station to get the eleven o'clock bus. This way I'll make it back before curfew. A man glances at me as we're waiting in line. He looks me up and down. His eyes linger on my breasts. Arthur notices.

"Just be careful," he says as I'm about to climb on. "Just watch out. They're everywhere, you know, the wolves."

I smile. I've taken one step up the stairs of the bus. I lean forward abruptly and kiss him on the mouth. He pulls away slightly, his expression confused. I turn and climb onto the bus. The windows are tinted dark. I can't see his face, just the shape of him standing there. He waits as we back out of the station. We make our way downtown. It's night, but the sky's illuminated, and between the buildings, the streets are alive. We veer once and then enter the tunnel. Sitting there in the dark, I lean my head back. I can still feel the pressure of his lips on mine. I think of the restaurant and the wine, Arthur standing at the bar, the bar itself, and the dark, snowy streets. I remember the way I talked in the bar. It's like watching another person, a girl talking in a bar. She wears a black dress or a green one. She could be anyone. And then I begin to imagine how it will be the next time I come, seeing him again.

I FIND ROE IN HER ROOM. SHE'S SITTING AT HER DESK, A VA-cant expression on her face that quickly disappears when I come in. "How was it?" she asks.

"Fine," I say. I'm still feeling a little loopy and drop down on the bed.

"Did you see him? Was he there?"

"Yes, we had dinner with a friend of his." I lie back. "And then we went to this bar, Roe, the nicest bar."

"Did you kiss?"

I smile, sitting up again. "*I* kissed him, right at the end. I think he wasn't really ready for it."

The warning bell sounds. Curfew is minutes away. I sit up. I don't want to go back to my room at all. I look around. There are clothes draped over the radiator and in puddles on the floor. *Moby-Dick* is open facedown on the bed.

"How was your weekend?" I ask.

Roe shrugs. "Fine." She smiles a bit wanly, puts out a hand. "I was here. I spent it here."

CHAPTER 5

"I INSIST THAT YOU COME," THE NOTE FROM MY GRAND-mother says. It's on that same cream-colored paper, monogrammed at the top. She's inviting me to spend Christmas with her. "And it's fine if you want to bring a friend."

I tell Roe. She's delighted. She, like me, was dreading going home for the holidays. "It just feels like you're taking a step back, doesn't it?" she says. "I mean, here when we've stepped out this far."

My grandmother lives on Long Island. Roe and I take the train past stretches of water, iced-over ponds. We arrive at dusk. The town looks abandoned at this time of year, parking lots empty and stores closed. My grandmother's driver, Marcel, is there to meet us at the station. He's as I remember, shy with kind, ice-blue eyes. We walk out to the car, black this time—the other one was silver—but with the same monogrammed doors.

The car glides smoothly through the deserted town and then beyond, into the darkness. We pass a golf course, cross a bridge, then bear to the right along a stone wall flanked by towering pines. The headlights trace the progression of the wall. We follow the road as it curves around—never have I been in a car so smooth—and then slow again as we come to a gate with a wrought-iron archway above it. We turn in. The drive seems to be made of thin gravel or clay. What you can see in the headlights is uneven ground. Giant firs rise at designated distances. Roe and I peer out the window. The headlights light on a birdbath with a scalloped edge. Then the house appears. It's large and white with several brick chimneys rising from its roof. But we see only a glimpse of the greater picture, what the headlights catch. Then we're too close. Marcel stops the car and we climb out. We follow him up the steps onto the front porch. There's a lion-claw knocker. He knocks twice and opens the door.

A beautiful young man with gold curls steps forward to greet us in the front hall. He wears a white shirt, has a drink in his hand. "I'm Calvin," he says.

He takes our coats. We introduce ourselves. Marcel carries our bags up the stairs.

"Where are they?" a booming female voice calls.

Calvin smiles at us conspiratorially. "Come," he says, "I think your grandmother wants to see you."

He leads us through a doorway into a spacious room where a fire is burning high. My grandmother is standing before the fire. She holds a drink and a cigarette, its tip stained a deep pink-red. At her feet is a tiger-skin rug with the head still on it. She looks as I remember, only even more splendid, now that she's in her element. Besides the fire and tiger-skin rug, there are leather couches and chairs, glass and silver ashtrays, a glass and silver cocktail cart on wheels, a set of elephant tusks mounted on the wall. And photographs in silver frames of my grandmother, younger, in extravagant poses. She watches us critically as we approach.

I remember how, the last time I saw her, I was meant to shake hands and hadn't. I step up to her now. But instead of extending her hand, she inclines from the waist and offers her cheek. I assume I'm supposed to kiss it. I move my face in, but what if I'm not? Will it be an outrage if I do? Later, I'll learn what she means. You're not supposed to really kiss her cheek, just graze it with yours. I kiss it directly this time. I hear the sound and feel the slight wetness. I've already realized it's wrong. Roe steps up after me and does the same. As she's moving away again, we hear a growl. We both look behind us, startled.

"It's Louis," my grandmother says. "Remember Louis? I think he wants to say hello." The white dog with the flattened face emerges from behind the couch. He wears a collar with small silver spikes. "That's right, say hello. Say hello, girls." My grandmother seems to be talking in a different register, with a measure of hilarity in everything she says, yet it's all undercover, never acknowledged, or rather the idea that there may be another way of speaking is never acknowledged, so we feel as if we are, however unwillingly, taking part in a play.

I look at Louis, the cropped white hair and the pink skin shining through. He has two long white bottom teeth that stick up outside his gums and lips, the gums pink, a little loose, rimmed in black. The last thing in the world I want to do is touch him. I approach, but my legs hang back. I'm leaning over, reaching to pat him. He growls again, then barks.

My grandmother laughs. Her eyes fly to my dress. "What in God's name are you wearing?" she asks.

I color.

"Be quiet, Lacy," Calvin says. "She looks extremely pretty, and you know it." He turns to me. "She says that to everyone. She said that to me when I first arrived."

"Well, of course I said it to you. You were wearing a plaid coat!" Calvin, amused, helplessly lifts his hands.

My grandmother turns back to me. Her eyes narrow. She looks at my face and the rest of me. "In any case," she says, "you're much improved." Then, turning away, "Remind me to lend you some of my clothes tomorrow." She glances back quickly at Roe. "You, too," she says. "Marcel, the hors d'oeuvres! Now, what will you two have to drink? Champagne? Martinis?"

"Champagne," I say. Subdued, Roe nods in agreement.

Calvin goes over to the cocktail cart to pour us glasses.

"Sit down," my grandmother says. She's still standing. Roe and I obediently sit down on the couch. She lights a cigarette. "Do you smoke yet, girls?"

Roe and I look at each other. We nod. "Sometimes, yes," I say.

She offers us each a cigarette. "So tell me about this school. It had a very good reputation in my day. Anyone interesting there now? Any Kennedys?"

I look at her. I have no idea. "I don't think so," I say.

"You don't think so! Well, you really must inform yourself! There's a boys' school nearby, isn't there? Saint Nicholas? Are you in love?"

I look at Roe. It wouldn't be right to describe Arthur as a boyfriend. At the same time it seems that, in this context, the most important thing is to deliver, whatever it may be, even a complete invention, the truth being irrelevant and the dominant idea to entertain. What you absolutely must not do is dampen things.

"I *have* met someone," I say.

"Yes? Really? Tell us. Calvin, come, she says she's met a boy."

"Well, he's older."

"Better yet, a man," she says. "Is he rich?"

I'm taken completely off guard by the question. "Well, no," I say, "I don't think so."

"No good, then."

"Listen to you," Calvin says, shaking his head. "The zeal of the convert."

"Zeal of the convert—what in God's name do you mean? My family was never poor."

Calvin shrugs. "Poor, no. Who said poor? Your basic middle class."

"Middle class, indeed! We were never middle class." She turns to the mantel to sip her drink, looks over her shoulder playfully. "At least *I* wasn't." My grandmother points at Roe. "What about you?"

Roe turns very red. "Am I rich?"

"No, silly. Are you in love?"

Roe shakes her head, relieved.

"Good," my grandmother says. "I have some lovely men I want you both to meet."

Marcel comes out with the hors d'oeuvres. They're little, ornately arranged things, scallops wrapped in bacon, miniature sausages in tiny rolls. I taste one of the scallops. It's delicious and like nothing I've had before. Roe takes a miniature sausage.

"Is this man of yours handsome?" Calvin asks me.

I shrug. "I think so," I answer. "He's dark."

"Dark?" my grandmother asks. "Dark in what way?"

"His hair and eyes."

"Well, is he black?"

"No," I say, "he's Romanian."

"Romanian? My God!" She starts laughing. "And what in God's name is he doing here?"

I'm getting more and more confused. "What do you mean?"

"Well, has he immigrated?"

"He lives here," I say, "he's half American. His father's American."

"Good Lord!" my grandmother says. She sips her drink again. "So he's poor, he's Armenian. Let's hope at least he drinks." She looks at both of us. "Always make sure they drink. The ones who don't, like Richard, my second, are utter bores." She turns to Calvin. "Speaking of utter bores," she says, "where's that friend of yours?"

"Sleeping," Calvin says.

"Well, wake him up. Really! What kind of guest is he? Bring him downstairs. I don't care if he doesn't want to come. He has to prepare himself for our party. Marcel, go with Calvin and bring that man downstairs. I won't have anyone sleeping at cocktail hour."

Calvin and Marcel go upstairs. My grandmother disappears into the bathroom. Roe looks at me. She opens her eyes wide. "She's a trip," she whispers.

"I know," I say.

We hear thumping on the stairs, then Calvin's voice and that of another man, swearing. A moment later, Calvin and Marcel appear, carrying a man between them. He looks heavy, solid. He has dark, curly hair. They bring him into the room and lie him down on the couch. He's squinting and muttering. "What are you doing? What the hell are you doing?"

"Lacy!" Calvin calls.

"She's in the bathroom," I say.

Calvin goes and knocks on the bathroom door. "Lacy, we got Toby down here. Not without a struggle."

The man on the couch, Toby, opens his eyes more clearly. He's looking straight at Roe and me. "Who the hell are you two?" he asks. He manages to turn, to sit himself up. "What's going on?" He looks at Calvin accusingly. "Why did you bring me down here?"

My grandmother comes out of the bathroom. She has fresh lipstick on. "Give him a drink," she says.

Toby looks at her with disgust. "How can you live like this?" he asks. He gets up. His face has been smashed by the pillow. He looks like he's suffered. "You're still drinking?" he asks. "What a waste, I can't believe it! I feel disgusting, poisoned!" He shivers. "I've drunk more in the past two days than I have in the past ten years."

"He's definitely out of practice," Calvin says.

"Well, he better start training," my grandmother says. "How will he ever make it to New Year's Eve?"

"Oh no," Toby says, "I'm not staying for New Year's Eve. I won't survive. I won't leave alive. Why," he looks at her, "you must be completely pickled inside."

My grandmother throws back her head and laughs.

Toby looks at us. "And who are these girls?" he asks. "What the hell are they doing here?"

"It's Lacy's granddaughter and her friend," Calvin says.

"God help them." Toby stands up, goes over to the cocktail cart, and begins angrily pouring himself a drink. "You people are completely insane. It's repulsive, really." My grandmother lets out her booming laugh.

I WAKE TO ROE'S VOICE WHISPERING MY NAME. WE'RE sleeping in twin beds with pale-blue-and-white-striped covers on them. There are prints on the wall, of white men chasing Indians or the reverse.

The house is quiet. "I don't think anyone's up," Roe says.

We get dressed and creep quietly down the stairs. A gray morning light comes in the windows. It's late morning, ten o'clock or so, but the sky is sealed over with clouds.

There are glasses and ashtrays full, a burnt black log in the grate, not yet decomposed into ash. We look in the kitchen. It's in similar disarray. I open the refrigerator. There's nothing but a tray of rosy shrimp and red cocktail sauce.

"Should we eat this?" I ask. We hesitate, but we're hungry. There's nothing else in sight.

We take the tray of shrimp and the cocktail sauce into the living room. It's very quiet. Roe and I dip the shrimp and walk around the room, looking more closely at the photographs, in black and white. One is of my grandmother and several men lounging by a pool. Out the window in the gray light, we can see this same pool drained and covered with a blue tarp. In the photograph, my grandmother wears a bathing suit. She looks over, smiling, a cigarette in one hand. A man stands behind her, cut off from the shoulders up. Another sits beside her. He's looking not at the camera but straight ahead, his legs stretched out. He's thin and light, has a fine firm chest, with thin, light muscles.

Another photograph shows my grandmother in a dark coat and matching hat, the young mother. She's stunning. Below, on the ground, her hand lifted up to hold my grandmother's lowered gloved one, is a small chubby girl with a somber expression, dressed similarly. I lean nearer. The girl is my mother. It seems incredible. I look into the chubby girl's eyes. She must be five or six, but she looks very small, or maybe it's that my grandmother in high heels towers above her, the girl's face just clearing her mother's slender knees.

"That's my mother," I tell Roe.

"Really?" Roe asks. She, too, leans in to look.

Suddenly I stop, a shrimp midair. "Where's Louis?" I whisper.

"Who?" Roe asks.

"Louis! The dog!"

Roe looks at me, remembering, too. Both of us start giggling. How horrible it would be to come face-to-face with Louis when we're here in the house alone. We decide to go outside. We find our coats in the hall closet and softly step out the door. The lion's-paw knocker clanks slightly, then falls still. The grounds are surrounded by the stone wall we saw coming in. The land is uneven, in brief dips and mounds.

I tell Roe what my grandmother said about burying her husbands. I point to a mound and then to another in the distance.

"You think those are graves?" Roe asks incredulously, though half willing at this point to believe anything.

I laugh. "No," I say. "But can't you picture her, out here in the dark, digging graves for her husbands?"

Walking along the clay drive, we see more clearly what we saw the night before in the glimpses of the headlights, the tall firs rising. Frost, everywhere, covers the ground like gauze. In a clearing, we come upon the stone birdbath, its basin full of ice. Farther on, creeping from behind a shorn lilac bush, is the firm black body of a porcelain panther. Behind the house, the glazed, hilly ground falls to the pool below. We follow it down. The blue tarp glows in this gray day. Around the pool is a miniature sidewalk, and to one side a latticed bathhouse.

Roe and I look inside the bathhouse. A Styrofoam lifesaver hangs from a hook beside a rumpled woman's bathing suit. I remember the photograph of my grandmother with the men around the pool. I picture her stepping in here with one or another of them, conducting secret affairs.

We walk around the pool. Ice has collected along the wrinkles of the tarp. At the far corner, mounted on a pedestal, we come upon the bust of a girl. It's that same girl, my mother, from the photograph, though a bit older, nearing adolescence, the same full face and solemn expression. My mother, watching over the frolickings around this pool. Does she know she's here? What would she think if she knew? I'm sure she wouldn't be all that pleased.

Roe and I stand shivering at the pool's edge. The frosty air seems to have crept into our bones. Yet we don't want to go inside and face whoever might be there. Then a figure appears, coming around the side of the house. It's Marcel. He heads toward us down the hill. He wears a wool shirt but no coat. He's shivering, too, rubbing his hands.

"Did you have breakfast?" he asks, arriving.

"We had shrimp," I say.

"Shrimp?" he says. "Oh, yes. I've built a fire. I can make you some eggs. Why don't you come inside? No one's up," he adds, as if guessing why we'd hesitate. Roe and I look at each other, tempted to stay outside. But the fire and hot eggs sound so appealing that we look at Marcel gratefully and follow him in.

As the afternoon draws on, the figures from above stumble down one by one, first Toby, then Calvin, then my grandmother. Toby and my grandmother look overwhelmed, their faces laid waste. Calvin's fresh face is only slightly drawn, but he moves with a heavier step.

"Don't look at me," my grandmother growls as she enters the room.

THAT DAY, AS PROMISED, MY GRANDMOTHER PUTS A LARGE pile of her throwaway clothes on the twin beds, silk shirts with Chinese fastenings, suede pants, camisoles smelling of her perfume, even a box of jewels. There's a dressing table in our room, painted white with a mirror in the center and a low set of drawers on each side. Roe and I try on the clothes before the mirror. We mix my grandmother's things with ours.

"Look," Roe says. She has a silk shirt on with some of her own men's pants and diamond earrings in her ears.

When evening comes, Roe and I get dressed in front of the mirror. We try on everything all over again, waiting until it feels just right. Roe wears a pair of suede pants and a silk shirt. I decide on a pale gold silk dress with Chinese fastenings. Then we go downstairs.

It's cocktail hour. A few guests have already arrived. My

grandmother turns from talking to someone. "There they are." She looks us up and down. "Much better," she says.

Calvin asks us what we're drinking.

"Make them martinis," my grandmother says before we have time to answer.

Standing there, Roe and I, in our beautiful clothes, holding martinis, it all feels pretend but at the same time real.

"Come," my grandmother says, "I want you to meet the Lawrence boys. And remember, everyone's interested in a young girl, so for God's sake, don't be shy."

The Lawrence boys have square faces, wear dark suit coats. They're twelve, eighteen, and twenty-two.

"How do you do?" Roe asks with her southern intonation. Her face, flushed from the martini, emanates a steady pink glow.

The two older boys are very gentlemanly. They ask Roe about being from the South. They ask me where I'm from. They tell us about themselves. They both go to Cornell College. One is a sophomore, the other just graduating. He hopes to start working at a bank. The twelve-year-old has his eye on the checkerboard.

I watch Roe listening, her face bright and blank. She looks so strange in her fancy clothes and at the same time so familiar, and the boys, in comparison, seem of no consequence whatsoever. We can say anything to them, I think.

I turn to Roe. "Didn't Fred go to Cornell?" I ask.

She pauses for a second, then picks up my tack. "Yes," she says, trying not to smirk at the choice of the name.

"Who's Fred?" the older of the brothers asks.

"Her boyfriend," I say.

"No," Roe says quickly, "not anymore."

"What's his last name?" the boy asks. "Maybe I know him."

Roe misses a beat. "Chair," she says.

"Chair? Fred Chair?"

I turn away, giggling.

"Yes," Roe says, "funny name."

I turn back. "It's actually spelled 'c-h-è-r-e,' like the French, but pronounced 'chair,' " I say.

Roe, at this, can hardly contain herself. But both boys nod helpfully. The twelve-year-old has wandered off to play checkers alone.

"So you and this guy broke up?" the older brother persists.

"Yes," Roe says, looking down at her hands, "last year."

"I'm sorry to hear that. Had you been going out for a while?"

Roe shrugs, looks at me helplessly. "A year and a half." I'm watching and smiling. "A little bit longer than you and Raoul," she adds.

I laugh out loud at the name Raoul. "Why are you laughing?" the second brother asks.

"Just because," I say, still laughing, "my boyfriend hates it when she calls him Raoul."

"What's his real name?"

"Ralph."

The conversation continues for a while in this vein, Roe and I picking up where the other leaves off, elaborating on each other's lies. It hardly matters to us what the boys themselves say and even whether they believe us. It's as if Roe and I alone are illuminated, standing here together in our fancy clothes, and the rest of the world

[99]

shadowy, the boys and the other guests, the room, the fire and the rug, even Calvin and my grandmother, barely seen or heard.

CHRISTMAS IS A QUIET AFFAIR. JUST TOBY AND CALVIN ARE there. My grandmother gives Roe a hundred-dollar bill and me a ring with a diamond and an emerald. She goes to bed early. The fire burns low. The party, the real one, is reserved for the New Year.

Midway through the afternoon of the thirty-first, the house still dead apart from Marcel and us, there's a light knock on the door. Roe and I are seated near the fire, reading. Marcel has gone into town to buy the last things for the party. The knocker raps again. I go to answer. There's a young woman outside, perfectly groomed. She's in her late twenties. She looks absolutely lovely and perfect in every way, and surprised to see us, but not too surprised. She looks like she couldn't be too surprised by anything.

"Hello," she says, "is Lacy in?"

I nod. "She's asleep, though."

"Oh," the girl says, "typical," passing by me and walking in. "And Marcel's not around?"

"He went to town," I say.

She clearly knows the house. She puts her coat in the closet, glances in the hall mirror, giving herself the coolest look. Then she turns again to me. "I'm Muriel, a friend of Lacy's," she says. "Are you here for the party?"

"She's my grandmother," I say.

"Oh, really?" She arches a perfectly shaped eyebrow, looks at me with more interest. She really is lovely, with shining black curls, slightly full cheeks. "Well, that's something," she says. She walks into the room with the fire. "And who's this?"

Roe stands. I introduce her. Muriel moves on into the kitchen. She does everything as if by impulse, moving quickly, her shiny black head darting about like a rare species of ant. We both follow, drifting behind her. "If there's anything I can't stand, it's a morning-after mess," she says. Next she heads for the stairs. "I'm going to wake her up," she says. She turns. "Are there other people here?"

We nod.

"Who?" she asks.

"Calvin," I say, "and his friend Toby."

"Oh, Calvin," Muriel says, rolling her eyes. She goes on. We hear her in the hall, her brisk movement and bright, blunt voice. "Everyone up," she says, "up, up, up!" She knocks on doors. There are groans. Then we hear her going into my grandmother's room. "Lacy, up, up!"

More groans. Then a muffled voice. "What in God's name are you doing here, Muriel? You were invited to a party. No one asked you to come in the morning."

"I drove up early. I thought you might need help. You clearly do."

Roe and I return to the living room. In a way that we've witnessed numerous times before, the figures from above, in various states of mood and mind, one by one emerge. Muriel circles around them busily, commenting, scolding, distributing coffee. It's four o'clock.

Three hours later, the party begins. My grandmother looks stunning again. She wears pants, jewels, and her gold shoes. The Lawrence boys are there. Roe is talking to the middle one. There are new faces, an Austrian couple, a woman my grandmother's age with her husband, a doctor. Muriel entertains, darting about. She pairs people up; if the hors d'oeuvres tray is empty, she promptly signals to get it filled. My grandmother is quite oblivious to all this, Muriel and Marcel working as a team. Calvin stands beside the bar, shirt open at the neck, with Toby beside him morosely drinking away.

My grandmother leans in to me. "Your mother missed out on all the fun in life, living out there with her vegetables. It's drab, drab! And the drab clothes she wears." She fingers the collar of the silk shirt I'm wearing, one of hers. "You look lovely, darling. Come, there's someone I want you to meet." Taking my wrist in her hand, she leads me across the room. "He's terribly attractive, an expert on safaris. I've told him about you."

The man in question is in his forties, with a large frame and curly hair tight to his head. "Are you teaching your granddaughter the lessons of life?" he asks as we arrive.

"Of course. 'Give me a girl at an impressionable age—'" my grandmother says. She introduces us—the man's name is Stan—then moves away.

"She's an extraordinary woman," Stan says, watching my grandmother go. He seems delighted by the idea that I'm her granddaughter. He says he's heard that she's sending me to school. He asks questions about the school. I don't want to disappoint him. I'm sure I'm saying all the wrong things. But he doesn't seem to mind. There's warmth in his face, in his eyes. And all along I'd thought it mattered what you said to people. But he seems delighted by anything I say.

I escape to the bathroom. But as soon as I come out, his eyes follow me again. Maybe my grandmother's right, I think. Everyone *is* interested in a young girl. I look at my grandmother across the room, standing in a circle of men. She leans in, her feet in the gold shoes planted somewhat wide, then reaches out and, bracing herself on the nearest man's shoulder, throws her head back and laughs. Watching her, I feel myself picking up on the vein of hilarity, or being picked up by it. The Austrian man is down on his hands and knees, searching for something on the rug. Muriel has dropped an earring. She watches from above, only mildly perturbed.

Hours and several drinks later, I look around for Roe. She's nowhere in sight. Maybe she went to bed. I go upstairs and look in our bedroom, but it's empty. I pause before the window, peering out at the dark empty yard, then go back downstairs. I check the kitchen—she's not there—and begin to look in the other rooms. One door is closed. I open it. There are bodies on a couch, fumbling. It's dark, but the open door throws in a rectangle of light. It blanches a face, Roe's, and then another, the middle Lawrence boy's.

"Oh, sorry," I say.

I hear Roe giggle. I go back into the living room. The voices are hushed. Everyone's eyes are turned to the center of the room, where my grandmother is dancing very playfully with the oldest Lawrence boy. She has one gold shoe off. Now she kicks the other one high. It hits the ceiling, then falls, breaking a glass. She moves her hips lightly, laughs. The young man spins her around, barefoot now. He makes her dip back. A button on her shirt pops open. He reaches over and unbuttons the next one down.

Stan's watching, enchanted. He catches my eye. I feel a little dizzy. I go into the kitchen to get a glass of water. Stan follows. I don't know he's behind me until I turn around. I look at him. He still has that enchanted look. I do a few dance steps, too. He laughs, delighted. He comes toward me. He takes my hands and kisses them. "You're a lovely, lovely girl."

He leans in and kisses me on the lips. I let him. Then I kiss him back. He puts his hands on my waist, grips my waist. His touch is urgent. I think of Roe and the boy in the other room.

"Can we go somewhere?" he asks. "Can I take you for a drive?"

It occurs to me that this could be it. I'd almost just as soon get it over with. Then I think of Arthur, his forehead, and how it felt kissing him.

Just then Calvin enters the kitchen. "Oh, dear," he says. He's come to fill the ice bucket. He takes a step back.

"No, no, it's all right," Stan says, ushering him in, both flustered and annoyed.

Before Calvin disappears again, I take the opportunity to slip off to my room.

THE NEXT DAY, AS ROE AND I ARE LEAVING, MY GRANDMOTHER comes down in the early afternoon to say good-bye. She's in her dressing gown, her hair awry, her eyes dark and somber. Like the room around her, she has a gray look, as if all the brilliance of the night before has disintegrated into ash. And suddenly it all seems a bit absurd, the elephant tusks and photographs, the dead tiger, all the paraphernalia of her splendor. She's slouched in her chair. We're standing, already in our coats.

"It's quite clear that you girls are all grown up," she says, lighting a cigarette. She looks at me. "Next we'll think of college. Your mother went to a lovely college."

There's silence in the house. She seems strangely at a loss for words. "Where is everyone?" she asks. "Where's Muriel? Where's Calvin? Marcel!" There's no answer. "Goddammit!" she says. "Marcel's taking you to the station, isn't he?"

"Yes," I say, "I think he's putting our bags in the car."

"All right, good." She sits back again. "Did you have a nice time?"

We nod. She looks away out the window. She seems to be thinking back on the party, enjoying her reflections. "Yes," she says, "that was great fun." She must be picturing herself dancing in the middle of the room, everyone's eyes on her. She almost seems to have forgotten us entirely. Then she remembers. She turns to me, her face softer.

"Now you go back to your poor Romanian, hmm?"

When Marcel comes in, my grandmother gets up and walks us to the door. Her legs seem wobbly. It looks like she's placing her feet slightly wide apart for further balance, as if otherwise she might fall. She bends stiffly to take our kisses, pats me on the back.

"Tell your mother we missed her," she says.

CHAPTER 6

JASPER CALLS ME AT SCHOOL. HE SAYS HE MISSED ME AT Christmas. Always before, we'd go out in the woods together, find a tree, and cut it down. I ask him what he did instead. He says he spent Christmas Eve alone, then the next day went to the neighbor's. The idea is crushing, I can't bear it, Jasper alone and then at the neighbor's, people he barely knows. I quickly begin telling him about my grandmother and her friends. I describe them all, imitate her. As I'm talking, it occurs to me that Jasper's the one who taught me how to do this, tell a story, act out the characters. Now he laughs, enjoying it fully. Once I finish, there's a pause. I feel a sudden urgency to get off the phone. But he goes on. He says he's been thinking about me a lot. He's begun to think that something's happened, since I never call or write. I've met someone, haven't I? Fallen in love. I'm evasive. Why don't I tell him? Who is this person? Where do I meet him and when?

I hang up finally, all the more determined to go through with my plan.

I CALL ARTHUR AND SAY I'M COMING TO THE CITY AGAIN. I invite him to meet me for a drink. On the forms we filled out at the start of the school year, I put Jasper down as my stepfather. I also know how to do his signature. I compose a false note in his name, inviting me to stay over in the city with him and give it to Mr. Ryan.

On Saturday I get dressed in my room. I look in the mirror. I have in my mind what I plan to do. Roe knows, too. I told them at my grandmother's that Arthur was my boyfriend, and I'm determined to make the truth match what I've said.

The ride in, the dusk falling out the windows, it's winter, the landscape changing, the world of trees and fields transforming as we go into this other world—of pavement and streets, grays and blues. We come out of the tunnel, swerve upward. The lights along the streets are going up, going on. Next we're skirting the park. We're getting into familiar territory, upper Broadway, the restaurants and shops, I recognize street corners, and now figures in the streets, the boy from the Dominican diner unlocking his bike, the bag lady lounging on a piece of cardboard, she doesn't even feel the cold.

I had always thought I needed to confront my fears, walk right into them. I had thought I was doing precisely that, only now the fears themselves seem to have evaporated. It's a heady feeling, there's nothing there. I seem to have walked straight into thin air.

Arthur has given me the name and address of a bar. It's large and airy. The tables have a purple sheen.

I arrive first and order a martini. Arthur comes later. He sees me from across the room, approaches. "You look different," he says as he's sitting down.

"I do?" I know I do. I feel different. I'm wearing my grandmother's clothes mixed with mine.

"What are you drinking?" he asks.

"A martini," I say. He raises his eyebrows. I light a cigarette. I take a puff, sip my drink.

He looks at me and smiles. "You have all the accoutrements," he says.

He asks me about my Christmas. I describe it, imitating my grandmother.

He laughs. "Is that the way she talks?"

I nod.

"So," Arthur says a moment later, pausing, curious, looking at me in a new way, "what do you plan to do when you finish school?"

"My grandmother says she wants to send me to college," I say. "And Roe and I want to travel."

"You do? Where?"

I shrug. "Everywhere. To Europe and South America to start with. Roe's first choice is Brazil."

He leans back, nodding, watching me. "And how will you pay for that?" he asks.

"We'll find a way," I say.

He really is looking at me differently. I can't tell if he's impressed or just overly surprised.

The bar grows darker, smaller, warmer. We have another drink and talk some more. In the bathroom mirror, I look at myself, amazed. What I can't believe is that he actually accepts it, that I'm really this person, sitting here conversing. It's like in those dreams when you don't fall but fly. Are they arms or wings? But of course, wings!

The bar's closing. He gets our coats. He asks where I'm staying, and that's when I say it—"With you."

The streets outside are dark, ice-covered. It must be freezing, but I don't feel cold. We get in a taxi. Looking out the window, I forget about him entirely, the lights blurring by, everything closing, the lights going out one by one.

We get out of the taxi along a narrow dark street. There are apartment buildings with steps, small trees in the sidewalk enclosed by little iron fences. Then we're inside and climbing upstairs. Up and up and up, it makes you dizzy but not tired. I watch his hand as he's opening the door, not looking at me. His face looks almost grim. I feel like laughing. What's he so scared of?

The lamps in his apartment shed a deep yellow light. The apartment is small and somewhat crowded. There's a vague hint of dust, the furniture antique, carved in dark wood, mirrors, a bureau, a desk and shelves. It looks as if it all belongs in a larger place, a house with tall ceilings and large wide halls. Here it's crouched, hiding, shoulders bent, still beautiful but hidden from view.

I reach out to touch the wooden carving around one of the mirrors. "Where did you get this?" I ask.

"Oh," he says, "they're all my mother's things, from her Romanian family." He goes into the kitchen. I look around.

There's one main room, separated by shelves into a study and a bedroom. The bed is low to the floor. Before it is a large window, reaching nearly to the ceiling. The kitchen, narrow, with a small narrow table, comes off the study, then the bathroom in sky-blue tile.

Arthur brings out a glass pitcher filled with water. The phone rings. He looks at it, surprised, then goes to pick it up. He talks very briefly. "Thank you," I hear him say, "but I just got home, I think I'll go to bed." Then, "No, no, I'm alone."

He hands me a T-shirt out of the drawer. It's dark blue, very long. I understand that I'm supposed to wear it. This, too, strikes me as funny. I go into the bathroom. The T-shirt, when I put it on, reaches my knees.

When I come back out, he's already in bed. There's one lamp still lit. I lie down beside him. He turns off the lamp. "Good night," he says.

He doesn't touch me at all. I'm surprised. He's lying very stiffly. I reach out my hand and let it creep across his chest. I can feel his muscles under the skin. He's tense, too, but doesn't move. I let my fingers move farther, down to his ribs. He reaches up abruptly and takes my hand. "Let's just sleep," he says.

Sleep? I suddenly feel very confused. This possibility didn't figure in my plan. "Do you have a girlfriend?" I ask, after a moment.

We're both lying on our backs in the dark. "Well, yes, you could say that," he answers.

"What do you mean?"

"She's not living with me anymore, but she used to." He shifts slightly. "We've had some—difficulties, but we're still trying to figure out what to do."

"I think I know her," I say softly.

"Who?"

"Your girlfriend. I mean, I think I've seen her."

"How could you have seen my girlfriend?" He turns and looks over at me in the dark. "You don't even know who she is."

"No, but, I mean, I think I saw her with you one day in the diner. Does she have a blue coat?"

He sounds exasperated. "I don't know. She has lots of coats." He

[111]

sits up and turns on the lamp again. "Do you know how old I am?" he asks. He's squinting, but he looks at me as pointedly as he can. "Thirty-two."

I shrug, then persist even though I can tell he's irritated. "Have you had a lot of girlfriends?" I ask. I feel as though it's all over anyway—he's refused me after all—so it doesn't matter anymore what I say.

He laughs, both irritated and amused. "I don't know if I've had a lot of girlfriends. I don't make a practice of counting them."

"For example, how many do you have right now?" I ask.

He looks at me, not sure whether to answer my questions or not, then leans his head back against the wall as if giving up. "Well, I have the one you're familiar with." He smiles ironically. "And then—since, as I said, we're not doing so well—there's another woman I've been seeing, on and off."

"What's on and off?"

"Once every two weeks or so."

"Who else?"

"No one else," he says, laughing. "Why do you want to know?"

I shrug. "I'm just curious."

He turns to me. "Listen," he says, "I like you very much. But that doesn't mean I want you to be my girlfriend. And I don't think you actually want me to be your boyfriend, either." He smiles. "I think you're just curious, exactly as you said."

He turns off the light again. "Good night," he says a second time, but I don't answer him. He reaches up to smooth my hair back from my forehead. It feels nice, but I don't respond. I feel not only confused but also ashamed. I want to leave immediately. I picture getting up and putting on my clothes. And then what? I remember the empty streets and the shadows along the edges of the buildings. The room is dark, the pillow deep and soft.

I'll go in a minute, I think.

I WAKE AND REMEMBER IMMEDIATELY. IT'S LIGHT OUT, I CAN tell, though I keep my eyes closed. I lie very still and listen. Arthur isn't beside me, I feel sure. I don't hear breathing. But he can't be far. I don't want to face him. I see my clothes in a little pile on a chair. I could get up, put them on in a flash, and slip out the door.

There's no sound. I lift my head and listen. Still nothing. Very, very quietly, I sit up and look around. The sun sends in a glaring light. I listen toward the bathroom—nothing. I stand up. The floor against my feet is cold. I walk carefully toward the kitchen. No one. I look at the clock. It's twelve-thirty. I go into the bathroom and wash my face, then come back out and get dressed quickly. Just as I'm about to step out the door, I hear footsteps on the stairs. It's him, I'm sure of it. Now what? I'll have to look him in the face, we'll have to talk, I'll have to feel ashamed all over again. Oh, why couldn't I have woken earlier? Then I would've been gone by now.

He's at the door. He's been out to buy milk. He comes in, looking agitated. "Are you sure you want to do this?" he asks. "Are you absolutely sure?"

I'm confused. For an instant, I don't want to. I feel a flash of fear. Then I remember that this is what I came for.

I nod. I put down my bag and take off my coat.

[113]

We say nothing. He undresses me and I undress him.

His body, the sight of it, startles me at first. It's much more beautiful than I'd imagined, the shape of it, its knottiness, the shadows in his skin. It astonishes me, his beauty astonishes me, the shape of his hips, the light, sharp bones, the way his torso grows out of them, widening, like a root or the gnarled trunk of a tree.

He's lying on the bed. I'm kneeling. I look and then reach out to touch him. I touch him slowly, marveling. It's like touching something marvelous, entirely new. He lets me touch him. While before he had a wild look, now he looks different, his eyes hooded over, as if he's been drugged.

He puts his hands lightly on my waist, skims my breasts, as if nothing more is allowed. Then, instead of his hand, he puts my own hand between my legs. "You know how to, don't you?"

I nod, embarrassed, then go ahead. He watches me, helps me, tucks my hair behind my ear when it's in the way.

"Keep going," he says, "you can keep going."

I go on. I feel my whole body growing rosy, flaring up, flushing.

I reach to touch him again. Again he asks me, "Are you sure you want to do this?" His voice sounds different, rough. This time, he's the one who's afraid. I see it on his face.

"Yes," I say.

Outside, the city passes by, I can hear it, the stops and starts, the whoosh of cars, the tap-tap of footsteps, voices rising, falling, and beyond that, a great muffled clanking, a low-level roar. I feel it all rise up in me. It strums in my ears.

At first, pain. And then something else that lifts the pain away, or drowns it, a wave, draws it out and under.

Afterward I have that woozy feeling you get at the end of summer when all the smells, fruit, earth, flowers, are beginning to turn from sweet to rotten and are overwhelmingly strong.

"Are you all right?" Arthur asks.

"Yes," I say. I feel a little sore.

The light is bright. He gets up and closes the blind. I lie there listening rapturously to the city passing by.

BACK AT SCHOOL, I GO DIRECTLY TO ROE'S DORM. SHE'S NOT there. Then I think maybe she's waiting in mine. She's not there, either, and I leave my bag. I go out to find her. It's Sunday afternoon. I check the library, then the dining hall. She's not there. Maybe she's out walking around the pond. I go out to the pond. I have the same clothes on I was wearing in the city. There's still snow on the ground. It soon wets my tights and shoes through. I stand at the edge of the pond and look out. I can see the path all around—empty. Then it seems obvious. She's gone into town.

I pass the chapel on my way to the road, glancing at the bench— she's not there. The light is beginning to fade. The snow seems to emanate a cold, clear breath. Fresh at first, it then feels chilling, even begins to sting. I head down the hill into town. My feet and legs are cold. Surely I'll meet her on the way up. But there's no one. The road is empty. I pass the first houses, crouched up high. Here and there a light goes on. The town, darkening on the outside, is lighting up from within. As I enter it, more and more windows start to glow. I look in the diner. The first people are eating their early dinners. The waitresses we know have gone home. Next I check the drugstore and the thrift store. The woman there is just changing her sign.

"Was my friend here?" I ask.

"Yesterday," the woman says, "she bought the prettiest little box. But today, no, I haven't seen her." She hesitates, her hands hovering ever so slightly. She glances down at what I'm wearing, my tights and dress. Is she approving? I can't tell. Her eyes settle on my face, curiously, kindly. But I hardly care just now. I can't think of anything but finding Roe.

"Thank you," I say, "I won't look today." I shoot a glance into the room out of politeness. "I'll come back later with more time."

I go back outside. Where could Roe be? I look down the hill to where the main street grows wider, leading out of town. It's dark. The light is gray. No one emerges. There's the bridge and the water below. I hesitate. Should I go down there? Would Roe be down there at this hour, on the bridge or by the railroad tracks? It's nearly past the time we're allowed to be in town. Should I look for her anyway? Suddenly, out of the dusk, a figure appears.

"Everything all right?" a voice says. It's Mr. Ryan.

"Yes," I say, startled.

"Are you sure?" he asks. He glances at his watch and makes a face. It's an exaggerated face, as is his tendency, but it still means something.

"Yes," I say, "yes. I'm just coming up." But I balk at the possibility of walking with him, out of shyness but also especially just now. "I'm waiting for someone," I say. "She's inside."

He nods and goes on his way up the hill. I wait until he's advanced a short distance, then, glancing back down the hill one last time, cross the street, and begin to walk up the other side.

My tights are hardened against my legs. My feet hurt from the cold. Where could Roe be? I walk faster. What could have happened? I picture horrible things happening. I've forgotten everything but finding her. Near the top of the hill, I leave the road and cut out across the snow. I'm running, taking the back way to her dorm. There's no one around. The snow crunches loudly underfoot. I see two dark figures walking in the distance under the trees. I stop. Is that her? It might be, but no. The height's wrong, the gait, the shoulders, everything. I pick up running again. In the distance, I can make out her dorm, the outside light glowing against the snow. And her light? I can't tell from this angle, only from the side. I veer sideways, still running. Yes, that's her light. I see a shadow. And that's her. Or is it? I run harder. Maybe it's someone else in her room. Maybe she's missing and they're all worried, looking. Sprinting, I arrive at the front door. I open it and pound up the stairs, one flight, two. I can't believe I'm still going, that I'm not tired. But if anything, my legs are lighter and stronger than ever. When I get to her door on the third floor, I knock but can't wait and barge right in. She's there at her desk. She looks surprised, almost frightened.

"Are you all right?" she asks. "What happened? What's wrong?"

I've forgotten everything that came before. I can't imagine why she's posing these questions to *me*. "What happened to *you*?" I say. "Where were *you*?"

"Where was I when?"

"This afternoon. I've been looking for you everywhere! I looked for hours in the library, in town, by the pond."

"But why? Are you okay? Did something happen?"

"No, no, I was just looking for you. Where were you?" I'm standing in the middle of the room. I feel scared and now almost outraged.

"I was here," Roe says. "For a little while, I was in the girl across the hall's room. We were doing the history assignment together. Are you sure you're all right?"

I nod. I sit down on the bed.

"And nothing terrible happened?"

"No," I say. I lie back, calming down, reorienting myself. The weekend with Arthur comes back. After a minute or two, I sit up and tell Roe all that happened.

THE COLORS AT SCHOOL, GREEN, BROWN, THE WHITE CLAP-board of the dormitories, the white-blue of the snow. The colors of the city, purple, gray. And drinks, too, their colors, gold and red, not like flowers but hard and bright.

I take the bus. This is the first step to entering the city. There are these moments of enchantment as I enter the city. The streets are gleaming and full of shadows. Lights have gone on in all the restaurants and bars. The memory of where I was this morning, in chemistry class, flickers across this setting where I find myself now. The reminder is essential, makes the scene what it is. For it is above all the contrast between tonight and this morning, the schoolgirl and this, which delights, enchants me.

Already on the bus, I can feel myself changing from one person into the next. It starts with the clothes and goes from there. I think about Arthur, his body, his skin, smooth and tense, the muscles beneath it clutching the bone. He lets me in when I arrive. I undress him. I make him lie down. He's smiling, watching me. It's a game we're playing. Maybe it's partially the way he behaves, casual, reluctant, that makes me desire him. He does nothing, or very little, lets me do everything.

Afterward, we go for drinks. There's the large, airy bar in the neighborhood where you can also eat. Mirrors hang along the walls like paintings. Arthur and I call this the Fancy Bar. We usually sit at a table. "That one, by the window," he says. He's always careful about choosing where to sit, always picks the best table, and if it wobbles, he folds a matchbook or a napkin and sets it right. Sometimes if the bartender is the guy Arthur knows, we sit directly at the bar. But we're cautious about this, because there was once a question here about my age. In the other bar we go to, there are never any questions and it's so dark anyway you can barely see. This bar is downstairs. In the window, there's a neon sign that says BAR in red letters. Behind the bar inside, there's a bust of Elvis. The bartender is very old and quiet and thin. It's always the same guy. If you stay late, he gives you one on the house. Arthur and I always do.

Arthur orders me drinks because I'm too young. When he was younger, he says, he used to drink a lot. Now he drinks only moderately. I drink every night I spend with him. Sitting there, I feel my mind growing sleek and smooth. And dark, too, but it's a lovely darkness, not still but alive, like great wings beating. I have my eyes on him, but I'm listening to the wings rising up, rustling.

A woman approaches our table. She knows Arthur, wants to talk to him. I nod, smile politely. I don't mind.

I know there are other women Arthur sees during the week while I'm gone. Women call and talk into the answering machine.

[119]

Sometimes he picks up the phone while I'm there. He says he's busy, he'll call later. But I feel that he ought to see other women whether I'm there or not, that I have no right to exert any claim on him. I even understand if he feels embarrassed by me; if, when we meet people he knows on the street, he pretends that I'm his sister, his friend, his sister's friend, a cousin he's met once, an unknown young girl passing through town, from the country, yes, or else older, a woman, a wait-ress in the restaurant he always goes to, a college student getting her MA. I feel that I can be any of the above, whatever the occasion calls for. I can adjust my expressions, my movements, my manner of speaking to portray any one of these things.

And I can also, when circumstances require, play this other part, the part of the young girl he sleeps with, aged fifteen to twenty, it's not quite clear but much too awkward to ask. As, for instance, one night late when we run into Lionel at the Fancy Bar. He's sitting across the room at a table with friends. He sees us, comes over, inquisitive, delighted. He looks at me in the same way as before, if not more unabashedly. Arthur hesitates, then reaches out, puts his hand on my hip as he speaks. Lionel's eyes dart from Arthur's hand to my face and back to Arthur's hand.

At first Arthur and I discuss general things, but little by little, in the bars we go to, he begins to tell me more. He talks about his fam-ily, about growing up in Europe, how his father had all kinds of schemes and went through all the money they had. How they were evicted time and again. His mother went along with his father's enthusiasms, kept hoping and, even after she'd lost hope, went along. He tells me that he fears turning out like his father. He's afraid he'll never finish this book. At the same time, he knows that he's more afraid of finishing it than of not finishing it. It's been years since he worked on it. What will he need to do to finish? I ask. Who knows? he says. The money he received to write it has run out. His editor calls every six months. They laugh. It's become a joke. Arthur looks very beautiful as he talks, and tragic. Everything fits with the image I had of him at the beginning, as Mr. Rochester, a man with a secret.

He says I'm one of those people nothing bad will ever happen to, nothing bad will ever touch me. I don't think it's true. But I let him believe what he wants to.

He also thinks I'm fearless. He says this fearlessness is partly due to my age. But that doesn't explain it entirely. It's also just me. I don't tell him that I'm actually frightened of everything, everything.

We go back to his apartment, climb the stairs, it's night. But the sounds of the traffic go on outside.

When I touch him, he moans. He doesn't touch me. Not at first. Then he does. He knows how to. Experience, he's done this before. This is what I want, what I've come for, his experience.

I want him to touch my breasts, to take them in his mouth. I lean forward. He takes them in his mouth, one and then the other. "Harder," I say. He sucks harder. And I feel, as he does this, a moment of suspension, of nothing, and then a lapping, spreading.

LATER, BACK AT SCHOOL, I LOOK AT MY TEACHERS, THE MEN, standing up in front of the class, and imagine I can get them to do that to me, too. When they step out from behind their desks, I see their bodies clearly through their clothes. I imagine that I could get them to do that to me easily, even those who'd try not to or who'd feel that it was wrong, I could get them to despite themselves. Not as myself, exactly, but as the person I've discovered I can become.

"But," Roe asks, "would you really even want to?" She looks at me, her expression wary, amazed. "I mean, would you really want to have sex with, say, Mr. Stein?"

Mr. Stein's the chemistry teacher. "No!" I say, flushing, "that's not what I mean." I break into a laugh that sounds high and crazy, full of relief. "Or maybe," I say, "that *is* what I mean." I grow quiet. "Or at least what I mean is something like that. Only the feeling's not related to what *I* want, but to the idea that I could make *them* want to."

Roe looks dazzled and confused. It occurs to me that what I'm saying may disgust her.

"I mean, I know that it's crazy," I add, "that it couldn't possibly be true. That I couldn't really force them. Or at least a part of me knows. But what's strange, and that's the reason I'm saying this, is that the other part actually *thinks* it."

Roe's eyes flicker, light. She's lost her wariness. "Yes, it *is* strange," she says, thinking. "I wonder why that is."

"It's as if," I go on slowly, "I feel that I could force them, only not as myself exactly, but as this other person I can become. It really is strange, this new feeling, that I can make myself become someone. It's as if," and as I say it, I feel myself illuminate, nervously, then brightly, "as if I've stumbled upon something quite by accident, a certain kind of power, to change myself into any form I please."

———

WHEN I RETURN FROM WEEKENDS WITH ARTHUR, ROE LOOKS at me as if she might not know me. She looks at me as if I'm suddenly strange. The sight of her strikes me as peculiar, too, as if her face may have been slightly rearranged, the features shifted infinitesimally. I feel anxious each time. Does this mean we'll lose each other? But then she begins talking in the old way.

One weekend, when I'm gone, she meets a boy.

"You did?" I ask, astonished. "Who?"

"He's from town," she says. "His name's Jesse." In her voice, there's a glow.

"How did you meet him?" I ask.

She was down by the river standing on the bridge. He crossed. They looked at each other. That was all. He went on walking, and then she did, too, in the opposite direction. She was going toward the railroad tracks. But then an hour or so later, she saw him again. She thought he might have followed her, but she wasn't sure. She hadn't noticed anything. She had been to the diner and the thrift shop. As she was walking back up the hill, he came up behind her.

"I turned and he was right there. He said hi. He asked me some questions. I answered but kept walking."

"What did he ask you?"

"Just—I don't know, if I was from the school. And if I liked it there. And then, well, at the top of the hill, I said I had to go back to my dorm. He looked disappointed, like he was expecting something else, I don't know what. Then he said he wanted to meet me again, to talk some more. And we agreed to meet the next day in town."

"On Sunday? And you did?"

She nods.

"And what happened?"

"Nothing." Roe's smiling. "But we kissed almost immediately." She's still smiling, but nervously. "He bit my lip." She shows me. It's still swollen, right along the bottom edge. "And then we walked around. He kept kicking things, like rocks or trash, as we walked. He grew up in town, or on the outskirts. He pointed out things, like a house off the alley where a friend of his lives. And he talked, my God," Roe says. She opens her eyes wide. "He talked nonstop. He gets very worked up about things, it seems, especially Ireland, the situation in Ireland, the struggle, you know, between the Catholics and Protestants. I guess his family's Catholic, not that he's religious."

"How old is he?" I ask.

"Seventeen."

"And he's in school?"

"Yeah, he goes to the high school in town. But he rarely ever goes." Roe shrugs and smiles. "He says it's all bullshit anyway, what you learn in school. He prefers to read the paper." She laughs almost foolishly. She seems not her normal self.

"And will you see him again?" I ask.

"Yes," she says, "Saturday. Down by the bridge."

And from then on, each week, when I get back from the city, Roe has more to tell.

"It's as if Jesse has some sort of obsession," she says, "only he isn't sure himself exactly with what. He seizes on things."

This time they had a fight over the weekend. It's Tuesday afternoon. She and I are walking down into town.

"In what way?"

"Just with everything. With his eyes"—she bulges her eyes—"and voice. He starts talking a mile a minute." She laughs. She clearly likes it. "He's talking a mile a minute, but at the same time, it's always interesting what he says."

"And the fight? I still don't understand what it was about."

"Me, neither. It started because he said of course I don't care about the situation in Ireland. Why would I care? I'm just a WASP, a privileged prep-school chick. I said how did he know? 'Look at you,' he said, 'just look at your face. And look at this.' He reached for my hair as if he was going to yank it."

"My God!"

"And I ducked and said the truth was that I was more like white trash." She laughs. "And that got him even madder. He was talking a mile a minute, and his eyes were bulging. We were in the alley. I didn't know what he was going to do. All I knew was that I wanted to get away. I started walking fast to get back to Main Street. He was following. I started running. There was that girl in my dorm, Anne, who was walking up the hill. She was pretty far away, but I actually called out to her, something I never would've done otherwise, but it was the only way to make sure I'd get away."

"And you got away?"

"Yes, yes. He stopped following."

"And you haven't talked to him since?"

"Yes, I did. We talked an hour or so later. He called and apologized. He wanted to meet. But I said that I didn't feel like seeing him. And then that night he came over to my dorm. I was sitting there reading, and I heard a scratch on the window. He was up on the fire escape, right outside."

"Roe!"

"What?"

"Well, he sounds sort of scary. And what if they caught you with him there?"

"Oh, they won't. It was dark and he was quiet. And he was also being nice, extremely nice, but I wouldn't let him in."

We walk for a moment, silently. We've passed the center of town and turned down a side street, heading nowhere in particular, walking just to walk. It's still cold, late February, but there's something else in the air, a current underneath, or else they're just spots, pockets of lighter, warmer air. Every once in a while, one breaks against your face. But then you enter a cold vein again. You think it's all imaginary, the warmer light spots, until, as you're turning, you feel one once more, like a bubble against your cheek, softly, lightly breaking.

I turn to Roe. "And you still haven't—slept together?" I ask.

Roe shakes her head. She shrugs. "No. He says he's trying to arrange it. He's trying to find the place. I mean, we've done other things. Under the bridge. It's nice under there, but cold. One day we even tried to build a fire. But no—he says he's trying to arrange something with his friend, the one who lives in town, so we can use his house. But it depends on the day, and if the friend's sister's there. It all sounds very complicated." She stops and takes a breath. "The truth is, as you can see, I have no idea. Not just about that but everything. I don't have the first idea of what he's thinking. I never know, when we're talking about something, if we're actually even talking about the same thing, I have no feeling whatsoever of being on common ground. It's a complete mystery. Utterly impossible." She pauses. Her eyes light. Then the words tumble out. "But completely intriguing at the same time."

We've taken another side street. The houses along this one are set back, with fences around them. The yards under the snow are sopping wet, dark brown, with spindly yellow-green strands of grass. Roe lifts her chin, seeing something along the street. "That's his friend's house." She points it out, a pale pink back wall. "That's where we're supposed to sleep together one day." We stop in front of it for a moment and look. There's a couch on the back porch with a gray cat on it. This yard, like the others, is sopping. We walk on.

The side street ends unexpectedly in a wide back road. This is where the trucks come through, but it's empty now. We've never been here. We're probably not supposed to be.

"Should we turn back?" I ask.

We both look out. The wide, empty road opens before us, alongside it wilderness, bulky tall trees.

Roe shrugs. "Let's walk a bit," she says.

I agree. We begin to walk along the shoulder of the road. Out of nowhere, a truck appears. It hurtles past. The sound is deafening. Our hair, coats, clothes go flying up, then settle.

"Should we turn back?" Roe asks.

I shrug. I think I see—or am I imagining it?—high up on one of the trees, the first green swellings, the buds of leaves. "Let's go on a bit," I say. We walk on, farther over in the grass.

"You know, it's funny," Roe goes on. "I mean, I *do* think it's impossible, and even sometimes disturbing, but I feel on the other hand so happily shaken up."

I nod encouragingly. "You do?"

"Yes."

"And that's what you wanted."

"Exactly. It's amazing." She lifts her face serenely.

Another truck whooshes past. I watch Roe's hair fly up, her coat, cuffs, skirt all flapping.

CHAPTER 7

ARTHUR'S GONE FOR A WEEK, A TRIP TO VERMONT, INTO THE mountains. I can't bear the thought of staying at school all weekend and decide to surprise him on Sunday when he returns. I ask Roe if she wants to go into the city with me on Saturday. She can't—she's already made plans to be with her boy. I determine to go on my own.

As usual, I write a fake note from Jasper and give it to Mr. Ryan. The day I'm leaving, I receive a postcard from Jasper depicting a nude, Manet's *Olympia*. "Thinking of you," the card says. I put it away in the drawer of my desk, then take it out again and put it in a shoe box in my closet where I store things. What am I afraid of? That it will be seen, misunderstood? Or maybe I'm afraid of misunderstanding it myself. I pack a small bag and get on the bus.

In the city I head, as always, to the same place. There's a small hotel at the end of Arthur's street. I've noticed it before. I get out of the taxi in front of Arthur's building and walk hesitantly down the street. I look over my shoulder as I'm entering the hotel. I don't know who I'm imagining would see me or, if they did, what I'm afraid they'd think, but in my mind the precaution seems necessary all the same.

The hotel lobby is small and carpeted, infused with an artificial orange light. There's an artificial wood counter with a woman behind it. I walk up to her.

"Yes?" the woman says. She's looking straight at me. I feel suddenly confused. It's the first time I've stayed in the city alone. Before I was either with Roe or here to meet Arthur. Now, alone, I feel like an impostor and am sure that someone will find me out. "What can I do for you?" the woman asks when I still haven't answered.

Finally, I get it out. "I'd like a room." Although the words themselves are pronounced correctly and all make sense, the rhythm of the sentence comes out flat-footed, all wrong.

"Excuse me?" she says.

I think I've completely misunderstood. This is not a hotel at all. "Is this a hotel?" I ask.

"Yes," she says.

I close my eyes quickly, then open them again. "I'd like a room," I say. I enunciate very clearly. I'm sure the woman won't understand me, or if she does, she'll tell me I can't possibly stay here—I'm much too young, or there's something else wrong with me. But instead she looks at me blandly.

"Will that be a single or a double?" she asks.

"A single," I say quickly, before she changes her mind.

"How many nights?"

"One."

"That'll be fifty dollars. You pay in advance."

I pull out the money I've accumulated from my grandmother's checks and count out fifty. The woman takes it and hands me a key. I can't believe it—she just hands me a key. It's squat and gold, Room 311.

"Call down if there's a problem," she says.

I take the small elevator to the third floor, then walk down the carpeted hall and put the key in the door. The room is dark and musty, everything, it seems, hung densely with cloth. The curtains and the bedspread are a dark paisley pattern. From the window, I can look out and see Arthur's window, farther down on the other side of the street. I look around the room. There's a bureau, knickknacks, a somewhat sunken bed. The bathroom is tiny, I can hardly fit in it, sink, toilet, and stand-up shower, all colored a dark maroon. On the walls are two paintings, one of a waterfall, the whitecaps on the falling water electric blue, another of a meadow full of what look like poppies.

Everything about the room is ugly, but everything pleases me all the same. I hang up my things in the closet, turn off the lights, and lie down on the bed. I lie there, listening. Dusk is deepening into night. Lights are going on in the windows across the way. There are noises from the street and then the closer sounds of the hotel's inhabitants. A man climbs the stairs. I hear gruff muttering and a dog. A woman's voice calls down from above. I get up to look at her from my window. She stands in her window two floors up, half dressed, shivering, calling to a man in the street below.

"Okay, okay," he says, looking up.

It seems she wants him to buy her a pair of panty hose and bring them up to the room. The man is reluctant, but he'll do it. I should get dressed, too, I think, and go out. But I wait. I don't want to yet. I lie down again, lingering.

The night darkens. The sounds change. I go on lying there. I'm not hungry. I'm not thirsty. I don't wish for anything. The dress I've brought is hanging in the closet. I picture it hanging there in the dark, quietly, waiting. Then I get up and put it on, black with lace. It fits perfectly, feels perfect. I put on my shoes and coat and go out, locking the door behind me. The woman downstairs is watching TV. It's the same woman, but she looks different now, friendlier, softer, her eyes and hair. She smiles faintly as I hand her the key.

"Have a good night," she says, her eyes drifting back to the TV.

I step out onto the street. The evening air is balmy. The trees, surrounded by little iron fences, are budding by the light of the streetlamps. Others, nearby, are already flourishing with leaves. I see a man coming toward me and remember—I'm alone. He walks past me. I hear his footsteps fading, and then I hear my own, the tap-tap along the sidewalk. I wonder if someone upstairs, lying down in a room, can hear them. I look around. It occurs to me that being in the hotel was one thing, but the street is another. Here I'm really in the world. I glance around again, more furtively. Now that I'm not with Arthur, surely these people will realize that I'm not one of them, that I don't belong here. When I reach the corner, I feel sure that someone will stop me, question me. What are you doing here? Where are you going? You're not supposed to be here. No one does. I stop at a newsstand and buy cigarettes. The man hands them to me without a glance. It's not the way people look at me, it's the way they *don't,* that thrills me. They seem not to notice anything strange about me.

I make my way to a bar. I pass the Fancy Bar, looking in cautiously and then going on until I come to the other bar, smaller, darker, the one with the pool table and no name.

I walk by once, peering in. It's hard to see anything; it's very dark inside. I walk by again. The bartender Arthur and I know is there, rabbity with horn-rimmed glasses. I caught a glimpse of him. Not that I've ever spoken to him, but he might, he must, know my face. Maybe I'll pretend that Arthur's joining me momentarily.

I step in, head bowed slightly. There's already a small crowd. I feel sure they'll all look up at me and laugh, or else fall silent. But nothing happens. The voices go on as usual. I look up. No one's looking at me especially strangely, no one seems surprised. Fortified, I step up to the bar. The bartender also doesn't seem surprised. Does he recognize me? I can't tell. It doesn't seem to matter. He asks me what I'd like to drink.

For the first time, I order my own drink, a shot of whiskey on the rocks, and carry it to a small table by the window. I take a sip and then another and then, lighting a cigarette, look up at the bar, at the people by the bar, at the pool table in the distance, the apparitions around it, materializing and disappearing. I look out the window at the view of the street. I'm at once excited and at ease. I feel fresher than I've felt all day, and more alive. My mind feels clear. It no longer distracts itself, thinks against itself, or brings up gnawing thoughts. Rather, it flows on sleek and smooth. I picture the bag lady sitting outside and the trees along the river flowering in the dark. I picture the water in the dark, and the grass, the silence under the earth in which the grass roots grow, in which, tiny pale shoots, they press out and down. I feel that I could sit here all night happily, at this table in the corner, sipping my drink.

Then, out of the blue, a man appears. He's standing by my table. He says he's been watching me from the bar.

I'm not sure what to say. This, other people, was not in my plan. He's bald, though still young, with pale clear eyes. He asks if he can sit down.

I agree. He seems excited that I agree, and more and more interested. He asks if he can buy me a drink. I say that I actually need to
get up early—I have a meeting—so I have to go after I finish this
one. He says that's a pity. Could he buy me a drink another time? We
plan to meet here at the bar the following evening for a drink. I
agree, though I have no intention of coming. I'll be with Arthur by
then.

I say good-bye and leave. Instead of going back to the hotel, I
turn down the street and go on to a different bar. This one has fish
tanks along one wall, glowing in the dark. One contains what looks
like a very small shark.

I take a seat by the window and order a drink. As I'm gazing out
languidly at the street, I see the clear-eyed man again, passing by on
the sidewalk. I pull back; he hasn't seen me. He turns a corner, disappears. My drink arrives. I light a cigarette. I sip it and settle back.
Something very pleasant ripples through my limbs.

The woman behind the hotel desk is dozing when I enter, but
she wakes. "Which room is it?" she asks.

I tell her, and she hands me the key. She says that if I'm leaving
tomorrow, I have to be out by noon.

I silently climb the carpeted stairs, silently go down the carpeted
hall, relishing with each step the thought of my room, waiting there
for me in the dark.

It is there, waiting, just as I left it. I turn on the lights and lock
the door. I sit down on the foot of the bed and look around. I look at
the paintings again, the whitecaps and the poppies. I look at the view
of the bathroom from here, the view out the window, of the night
and a streetlamp, the windows across the way. I turn off the light and

watch the reflections from outside moving on the walls. But I want to be entirely alone. I pull the curtains closed. Then it's just me and the room. I get up again and softly examine things, the drawer handles, the mirror, the closet, the curtains. I peek out the curtains, opening them a crack, then pull them to again. There's a TV, but I don't want it. I don't turn it on. I lie down again and stretch my arms up. The bed sinks in the middle. I let myself sink, too. I look up. There's a water stain on the ceiling to the left. I listen through the walls to the sounds of the night. Little by little, I drift off, deliciously, sinking, rising, sinking again. It's like being carried on soft ocean waves. At some point in the night, I don't remember, I get up and take off my clothes.

My confusion in the morning lasts only a second. Then I remember. I sit up and pull aside one of the curtains, then lie back again. I listen to the whoosh of a car pass outside, and watch a patch of watery light moving on the wall.

Noon approaches. I take a shower and pack my bag. There's no one behind the counter when I go downstairs, so, after hesitating for a moment, I simply leave.

It's a full spring day, warm in the sun, cool in the breeze. I have until five o'clock, when Arthur arrives. I walk along Riverside Drive. The park slopes steeply down toward the river. You take the stone steps, the long steep slope of grass alongside you. Then it levels. Along the mud path where the runners go, the fruit trees are flowering. Dogs are running wild. Others are on leashes. People are lounging on blankets on the grass. The Puerto Rican families have set up a volleyball game. They crowd together to watch and cheer. Babies waddle off on their own, to be chased and retrieved. There's a barbecue. The great wide river ripples beyond. I go over to the railing. The water is covered with glinting silver patches. Boats pass far out.

I walk over to the line of green wooden benches set up along the running path. People sit on them or lie down, faces to the sun. I find an empty bench and sit down, too. Then I lie back. I stretch all the way out, my face to the sun. The sun feels warm but not glaring. The Puerto Ricans are listening to music on the radio. The sun sinks into my skin.

At first, when people pass near—I hear their footsteps and voices—I glance up, lift my head. Who are they? Who knows what they might do to me, stretched out like this, eyes closed? Then I don't bother. I lie there, dozing. I think about seeing Arthur, how we'll do as we always do, make love then go for drinks. The wood of the bench underneath me is warm, the sun is warm, the breeze ripples through it.

After a while, I don't know how long, I wake and sit up again. People are passing on bikes, skateboards. Babies pass in strollers. I get up and walk, down past dog pens, playgrounds, a community garden, vegetables mixed with flowers. A man feeds the pigeons out of a plastic bag. They collect more and more densely, then flock up all at once, their wings shuddering against each other. I stop for a while in front of a young woman playing her violin. She wears a cream-colored Grecian dress. The violin case, tattered and brown, is open before her to collect change.

I have a quick meal at the Dominican diner, then walk over to Arthur's. I suddenly feel apprehensive as I'm approaching his building. I hope that by coming to surprise him, I haven't done something wrong. Maybe he's with someone? The thought, while disturbing, also interests me. What would happen then?

I ring the bell. He answers on the intercom. "Hi," I say.

"Maya? What are you doing here?" he asks.

"I was just in the neighborhood."

"Come up." He sounds surprised, but pleased.

He's waiting at the door when I get upstairs. I still have my fantasy that there's someone there with him. I expect to see her when I step inside.

No one. I drop my things on the bed. "You're alone," I say.

"Well, yes. What did you think?" He gives me a funny look.

We make love. I watch him, his drugged face, his torso, rootlike.

Afterward, we go out for drinks. He tells me about his trip. He thought about me while he was gone, even thought of calling. He went away with his manuscript, that was the plan. He didn't want to tell me before, in case he found he couldn't work on it. But he did. He read the whole thing through. It's better than he remembered. He's much closer to finishing than he thought.

He leans back. "So," he says, only half ironically, "it's the beginning of a whole new era."

I smile. "What will that mean?"

He's in a good mood. "You'll see before you an entirely new man."

"But I liked the other one," I say, playing along.

"Oh, no, no," he says, "this one will be better—" He interrupts himself. "Who's that?"

Someone across the room is blatantly staring at us. It's the man I talked to the night before, bald with pale eyes. He's sitting at the bar. When he catches my eye, he nods.

"Oh," I say, "just a guy I met."

Arthur seems ruffled, but amused. "Where did you meet him?"

I haven't told him that I've been here in the city since yesterday. Now I do. "I stayed in the hotel at the end of your street."

"You did?"

I nod, enjoying his astonishment.

"And you had a drink with that guy?"

"No, no, we just talked."

Arthur disapproves, I can see it in his face, but is also excited. This is the image he likes to have of me. And perhaps it's also the image I like to have of myself.

At night, in the city, and particularly if you've had a drink, you feel a certain courage. Your life is in the hands of strangers. This, right now, is where it begins. I feel this sitting here with Arthur, yet I felt it, too, the night before, in the bar on my own, this courage, this rapture, as if nothing in the world can match this or matter, in this city, in this night that will go on forever, and in which I will become, drink after drink, this person I have never known.

CHAPTER 8

ROE HAS HER WINDOWS OPEN AND IS CLEANING OUT HER room. Her hair is wet. She's just taken a shower. She's happy, excited to see me. She slept with her boy over the weekend.

"We did it," she says, "finally, and it was fine."

"But wait," I say. Her excitement is contagious. "Go back, tell me from the start."

"Okay," she says, "but should we go out? It's so nice." I agree. Roe flips a jacket over her shoulder, and we go together down the stairs. But she doesn't start talking until we're clear of the dorm, fearing, I guess, that someone will hear.

She begins at the beginning. They were at Jesse's friend's house in town along the side street, as they'd arranged it all along. It was raining, Roe says, but not heavy rain, rather the kind where the sky's still light. There were streaks of rain and the sun shining through them. She was nervous, had butterflies, not because they were sleeping together—she'd been dying to—but because they'd waited for so long. He was nervous, too.

"And not just nervous," she says, "but scared."

He'd prepared things, brought a little food and whiskey to drink. He offered her some whiskey. She didn't want it. That's when she saw that his hands were shaking. They were in the kitchen. He poured himself some whiskey in a glass and sipped it. Then he showed her the small bedroom off the hall. They peered in together. There was a single bed and a window streaked with rain. Jesse's hands were shaking less, but his face still looked scared. All Roe could think about was how to make him less scared. She lay down on the bed and reached out her hand.

"It was his first time, right?" I interrupt.

Roe nods. "Yes, I think so," she says, "but I didn't want to ask. I thought that would make him more afraid."

He came nearer. He seemed reluctant. He was still holding the glass with whiskey in it. She tugged at his hand. He put the glass down and sat on the bed. They started kissing as they usually did. He lay down.

Roe flushes. "At first it didn't work," she says. She looks down. "I was doing what I could. This went on for a while. He was getting more and more worried, I could tell, and frustrated. But I didn't know how much until he suddenly yelled, 'Fuck!' and punched the wall with his hand."

"Oh, no."

"Yes, and then he turned away from me. He had his face covered with his hand. I think he was crying. And then he got up and left the room."

Roe, her shirt unbuttoned, got up quietly to follow him. The hall was dark. He'd gone into the bathroom. She tapped on the door.

"Are you all right?" she asked.

"Give me a minute," he said.

Roe went back and sat down on the bed.

He came out. He looked sheepish, his face a little swollen. The rain had stopped. It was lighter outside, and you could hear the water dripping down on the grass.

They began again. This time it worked. Roe smiles, still triumphant. "I mean, it was very quick," she says, "but nice." She shrugs. "Or at least starting to be nice." She looks down again. "And I think he was happy. I mean, I know he was. And I was so relieved that it had worked at all. And that he didn't feel badly afterward. That's what I was most afraid of, that he'd feel badly."

The river in town is high with the spring rains. The water swells up, it rushes. Around the edges it eagerly furls. Roe and I stop walking and watch from the bank. It's lost its leaden color. Now it's a warm, hurried brown. It lifts off whole handfuls of mud, drags at the weeds along the shore.

Airy puffs of clouds fill the sky. Here and there in yards are brilliant patches of green, the daffodils and tall rubbery leaves of the irises. The tall leaves fall and fold from the weight of their tips. The stalks go on rising. The long colored buds are not yet open. You can only see a streak or two of brilliant color. But you feel that you want to see the whole thing, the full flower in bloom. You're tired of waiting. You almost want to pry the buds open with your hands.

Later, Roe and I are sitting under the copper beech tree, the light coming through the leaves green. In the grass all around is a buzzing and humming. Roe lies back, her arms above her head. I'm beside her, propped on an elbow.

"I think I always expect everything to be so hard," I say. "And then I can't believe it when it's not." Roe turns her face, her cheek a luminous green. "If something seems easy, I just can't believe it. I'm sure I've done something wrong."

"Really?" Roe asks. "What seems so easy now?"

"I guess just—life. I was so afraid of everything, people, the city, and suddenly it feels like it's all not that scary after all. Or"—I laugh— "it's almost as if we've conquered things."

Roe smiles. She's still stretched out, her arms limp above her head.

"I mean, look at you," I say, "look at you right now."

She laughs her high, watery laugh, gazing up at the ceiling of leaves. "I never thought of it like that, but I guess you're right. Think of all we've done—traveled, had affairs. What more is there to do?"

"Nothing!" I say. "We've done everything."

Roe's smile is wry. "Now I'm even feeling nostalgic for the way we were before, when we still had so much to try."

"Our lives are over, finished!" I laugh.

I walk back to my dormitory still laughing at what we've said. As I'm turning up the stairs, Mr. Ryan steps out.

"I need to talk to you," he says. He looks very stern. I wait for him to do as he usually does, change his manner entirely, turn this all into a joke, but he doesn't. He opens the door to his apartment. I step inside.

How often girls at school have pictured entering his apartment, his wife and kids gone. Now I'm doing it, but I'm hardly noticing. The circumstances are so different. "Is something wrong?" I ask.

He's looking away, scowling. He indicates a chair.

"We received a call," he says, "from a hotel. They claim that you took their key."

"I did?"

"I don't know if you did. That concerns me less. What does concern me is that you were staying in a hotel. What about this guardian of yours, Jasper Lewis? Wasn't the idea that you were staying with him?"

I nod, too shaken to think clearly.

"I've made some calls. I spoke to him myself. He doesn't live in New York and never goes there." He pauses. "So what exactly have you been up to?" I don't answer right away. "Don't bother telling me, I'm sure I don't want to know." He turns away. "This is wonderful, wonderful," he says. He seems to have gotten back a touch of his old mimicry. "Do you realize the kind of things that could happen to you? Do you have any idea?" I don't answer. He's getting more and more worked up. "And guess who'd be to blame?" He points a finger at himself. "You understand I'm obliged to report you, of course." I shrug, then nod. I hadn't really thought about it. "And that they don't take these things lightly here?"

I nod again numbly and go upstairs.

Once in my room, I sit down, stunned, on the bed. It's not so much that I feel worried, only wildly confused. It's like in a dream when two worlds collide. I look in my bag for the hotel key. It is indeed there. What was I thinking? And I remember, too, how I left this address when I was registering.

Over dinner in the dining hall, I tell Roe what happened.

"Oh no," she says, softly. She grew up getting punished by her father for things, and the idea frightens her. This might be the first time I've gotten in trouble in my life. I'm still trying to understand it.

"Did he say what they'd do?" Roe asks.

"Who?"

"The school."

"No, he didn't know," I say. "He said he'd find out."

My sleep that night is full of jarring dreams.

The next day as I'm coming in from classes, Mr. Ryan asks me once again to step inside. He says he's spoken to the people in charge. I have a meeting before the Disciplinary Board on Wednesday.

Going before the Disciplinary Board—it happens in a blur. The setting is a conference room in one of the administrative buildings, with long many-paned windows and thin carpet and a large wooden table so polished it shines like glass. Student and faculty jurors ask me questions. Then there's a half-hour wait while deliberations occur and finally the callback for the sentence to be pronounced. They say that the punishment in these circumstances for some would be expulsion. But Mr. Ryan has argued my case. In every other way, I've been a very good student. They've decided that I'm to be grounded for the rest of the year.

I call Arthur. He's there at home, working on his book. I tell him what happened.

"So that means you won't be coming to see me anymore?" he asks. He can't quite believe it. He sounds truly upset. I'm flattered, I hadn't expected this. "In that case, I'll have to come visit you," he says.

When I tell Roe the verdict, she's immensely relieved. A girl in her dorm was expelled recently for similar reasons. I should count myself lucky.

Saturday arrives, the day I'd normally be leaving. Roe, I know, is off somewhere with her boy. Out the window of my dorm room, the leaves are growing larger by the day, blocking up the chinks through which the light used to fall. Sitting there, I try to study but can't. I lie on the bed and try to read but can't. I get up and go outside.

I walk around the school grounds, then go into the library and sit down at one of the tables. It's nearly empty, only two girls at opposite ends of the room, heads bent. The rustling of clothes or the turning of a page sounds very loud. But I can't concentrate. I get up and go out again. I pass by the bench along the chapel wall, then walk over to the pond. I duck through the thickening leaves and look out. Several girls are in a rowboat on the water. Others are standing knee-deep by the shore or sitting out on the rocks in the sun. I recognize these girls. I know their names and certain facts about them, but not enough to say hello. They're all in groups. I'm embarrassed that they'll see me here alone.

I turn away and head down the hill into town. Here I can walk on my own without anyone noticing. But—I suddenly think—what if I run into Roe and Jesse? More than once I think I do see them, at the bottom of the street, turning down an alley or again just there, stepping out of the drugstore.

The light is failing. I go to the thrift shop, deciding to buy something new for my room. I haven't been here in a while. The woman looks at me familiarly, ducking slightly to peer in my eyes: Are you all right? she seems to say. How can she tell that something's happened? She smiles cautiously. I almost feel like sitting down and telling her the whole story. But there isn't an empty seat. I walk a few steps instead. Then I think, Why not just ask her for a chair?

"Do you think I could sit for a second?" I ask.

She quickly clears off a kitchen chair, with a blue vinyl cushion. "Are you tired?" she asks.

"A little bit," I say. "I'll just sit here for a second."

She smiles at me, as if I were less a person than a bird or some other type of animal brought in out of the cold.

I look around the room. She goes behind her register and busies herself quietly. I sit for a while, gazing out into the room, at all these things collected and sitting there together, very still. There are the bottles and glasses, the small paintings tilted up in frames, the snuff cases and jewelry boxes, the collections of jewelry, bracelets, brooches, and rings. My eyes fall over them. It's comforting. After a little while, I get up again. I don't feel like browsing. I choose one of the green glass bottles. It has square corners. The glass is greener in the corners, more translucent on the sides.

I pay for the bottle, thank the woman, and leave. I carry it with me up the hill, and put it on the windowsill in my room, where it catches the last fading light. It's dinner hour. Instead of going to the dining hall, I eat some food I've bought in town, apples and cheese.

But I still can't believe I'll be shut up for the night. I picture the night falling, the windowpanes growing darker and darker and finally just gleaming, revealing nothing but a reflection of what's inside. I look at the clock. I still have two hours before curfew and decide to go out again.

The windows in the dormitories are all lit up. Apart from the first few weeks, I've almost never been here on a Saturday night, and certainly not alone. I was always with Roe. Now I feel what I did back in the beginning, the blankness, the emptiness, of those days. I wander the darkened paths. Where is everyone? Every now and then I pass a group of girls, walking in clumps. I should approach them, say something. What, though? I walk by a window on the ground floor of a dormitory with a dark curtain hung over it, the music inside throbbing low. I smell a whiff of cigarette smoke. As I clear the wall of the dormitory, I have a view across the Green, of the chapel and, down the slope, the gym beyond. A stark outside light reveals clusters of people around the doorway of the gym, some standing still, others spilling in and out. I head over through the dark, with no intention of joining in, just to look.

I approach the gym, trying to keep in the shadows, then edge in to see what's going on. Music pulses inside. There are not only girls but boys, too. A dance with the boys' school. I've heard of these. Dare I go in? Mr. Ryan is in the doorway. I feel suddenly, paralyzingly, shy. Who are all these people? Is this what they've been doing on the weekends all along?

I peer in, step in gingerly. Girls and boys are dancing in the dark. Others crowd along the sides. They mill around, dressed in their favorite weekend clothes. The girls I recognize, have grown accustomed to, but the boys all look so young. The skin on their cheeks, hairless, like children's. Some, of course, are appealing already. Others are very awkward, with large Adam's apples, gangly limbs.

I stare for a moment. What if I stayed and joined them, danced? I look around. Everyone's absorbed. No, it's too late. I've cut myself off from this world. What right do I have to be here now? I turn quickly and stumble out.

I rush across the dark grass, leaving the gym behind. I head back to my dorm. It's still empty, except for several girls in one room, the door ajar, talking on the bed. I go into my own room, closing the door. But I'm still restless and wide awake. Why did I come back here? I lie down on the bed and stare at the ceiling, then get up again.

I empty my closet onto the bed and begin trying on all my clothes. I try on my dresses and look in the mirror. Something isn't right. A blankness has crept over my features. Is that it? Or is it the way I'm moving? I'm not moving, not standing right. Or maybe it's the setting. The dresses don't fit in this setting, or I don't fit in this setting with the dresses on. I try one after the other. Halfway through, I stop, though there's still a pile of clothes on the bed. I stare in the mirror. I stare and stare until I no longer recognize myself.

The bell rings for curfew. I hear the voices of the returning girls. Roe, I think, must be returning to her dormitory, too. I could, I suppose, call her. But it's already impossible—I can feel it—I'm already too alone. Shoving the pile of clothes aside, I lie down on the bed. I listen to the voices of the girls discussing their evenings. Little by little, they fall silent, close their doors. I lie there, still dressed. I get up, turn out the light, and lie down. I'm wide awake. I get up and take off my clothes, put pajamas on, lie there. The dorm is silent. The windowpanes gleam.

CHAPTER 9

ONE AFTERNOON, AS I'M RETURNING TO THE DORMITORY after classes, I find an envelope outside my door. It says "Maya" in Jasper's hand, but there's no address. How did it arrive? I go into my room and sit down on the bed, the envelope in my hand. I almost don't want to open it. As I'm sitting there stalling, I happen to glance out the window. There's a car parked in front of the dormitory, slate blue. I remember noticing it as I was coming in. It gave me a nagging feeling. Now I know why—it's Jasper's car, I'm sure of it. But that's impossible. I go out into the hall. I never knock on the other girls' doors, but now I feel I have to. The small girl with freckles is the only one here. She's in her room studying.

"Did someone come by for me?" I ask.

She nods. "A guy with a ponytail. He gave me a letter. I put it outside your door."

"Thanks," I say.

I go back into my room. The letter is on the bed. I really don't want to read it. But I go and pick it up. From where I'm sitting, I have a view out the window, so I can keep an eye on Jasper's car. I read the letter.

Jasper writes that he heard I was in trouble and wanted to come.

He knows I said I wasn't allowed visitors, and he wasn't sure he'd get to see me, so he's writing the letter just in case. He apologizes profusely for any part he may have had in getting me in trouble. It's the last thing in the world he would have wanted, as I know. Mr. Ryan was tricky when he called, not explaining until afterward what all this was about. Jasper says that he thinks about me a lot, that he's been having dreams about me, all kinds of dreams, even erotic ones, they took him by surprise, it must've been my voice the last time on the phone, there was something different in it. I must be sleeping with someone. Am I? More than one person or only that guy? He tells me the most recent story about Bella, how she got married while I was away, and then her new husband's brother fell in love with her. How the husband's brother would sit outside their house night after night, by the bedroom window, torturing himself, imagining what was going on inside. Jasper wants to know if I ever think about him. He invites me to come spend the summer with him in his new house, he has an extra room.

My hands are shaking when I finish. What should I do? I wait by the window, peering out along the edge. Jasper will have to return, if only to get his car. I'll hide, I decide. After a little while, I see him approaching from a distance. He looks scruffier and more boyish than I remembered. He's wearing work boots and colored clothes.

Seeing him almost makes me change my mind. There's the shuffling way he's walking, the expression on his face, innocent, expectant. But no, I can't speak to him. I hear him knocking downstairs, and hide in the closet. The small girl with freckles comes out of her room, goes to answer the door. When she knocks on my door a moment later, I don't answer. She opens the door and peeks in, then goes. I creep out and watch out the window as Jasper gets into his car and drives away.

I don't know what to do with the letter. I'm about to hide it in the shoe box with the card, but then decide to show it to Roe.

"My God," she says, "he's in love with you."

"No, no," I say, but my voice sounds dull. "It isn't that." I picture Jasper's expectant face. "It's just that he's confused."

ARTHUR CALLS TO SAY HE'S COMING TO SEE ME AT SCHOOL. He needs to speak to me. He's made plans. I agree to meet him in the inn just off campus where students' families stay. I suggest we pretend he's a family member, just in case. That's fine, he says, not to worry. He'll be very discreet.

On Friday afternoon, at the appointed time, I go to the inn. From the start, everything feels wrong. The inn is large and staid, with white columns marking the entrance door. Inside, it's decorated in mauve, with pale blue and green trim. There's a front desk and a lobby floating nearby with stiff parlor chairs, then a dining room to one side, and to the other a hall with elevators leading up to the rooms. I go into the dining room. It's mauve, too, with heavy mauve curtains and tablecloths and several chandeliers. I can't for the life of me imagine Arthur and me sitting there.

I decide to wait for him outside—maybe we can go somewhere else—but as I'm turning, I see that Arthur is already there. From a table in the corner, he raises a hand. There are two other tables occupied, the rest all empty. Arthur begins to stand as I approach. I feel wildly embarrassed. For him? For me? I can't tell. He looks so out of place. I'm in my uniform. The only other people there are students with their parents.

When I get to the table, Arthur squeezes my hand. The waiter brings us menus. They're very large, mauve, too. The meals listed are all basic, roast beef with potatoes. Just then an older man in a white shirt and black suit trods in, heading straight for the piano. He plays a few odd practice notes and trills and then, without missing a beat, begins to play smoothly, professionally, one song or snatch of song blending in to the next. Arthur smiles. I try to smile back, but I simply can't get comfortable.

"I have some news," Arthur says, once we've ordered. "I've made plans for us to go away together this summer. To France. You said you wanted to travel. It's nearly all arranged."

"What do you mean?" I ask. I'm confused, even frightened. He's behaving in a way he never has before.

"I've been working on my book," he says. "Just last week I went to see my editor. We talked about everything. She's very excited. We agreed that it would be perfect if I could do some last research, go look at some of these churches and cathedrals one last time." I nod, but I feel as if I'm only half listening or hearing him from afar. I'm too distracted. I glance toward the door. What if a teacher comes in? I feel uncomfortable about being seen sitting here with Arthur, even if he could easily be mistaken for my uncle, cousin, brother. All the same, it makes me edgy. "My editor's brother-in-law has a house in France, in the countryside," Arthur goes on. "She suggested that I go there and finish the book."

"When would we go?" I ask. My voice seems to be coming from a distance.

"This summer. We'd fly to Paris, then make our way down to the house, stopping here and there to look at things."

I'm picturing the landscapes, riding trains. Isn't that what I've always wanted to do? This time the thought makes me dizzy. I imagine myself clutching the train seat, holding on for dear life.

"It could be one of those magical times," he says, taking my hand, "the times you remember."

"Yes," I say. But my voice sounds artificial. What's wrong with me?

The piano-player keeps playing. The food arrives. As we eat, Arthur talks on about his plans for his book, for the trip, things we could do and see. He talks about visiting places he spent time in as a child.

I listen, nodding. But I can't get my bearings. I keep glancing at the door or down at my food. Finally we finish. Arthur asks for the check. I say I have to go to the bathroom.

When I return, Arthur is standing in the lobby. But it's as if a wildness has seized him. He's by the front desk, our coats bundled in his arms. His face looks almost stricken.

"I'm getting us a room," he says. He says it very softly, agitation in his eyes.

I'm so surprised, I don't know what to answer. I'm whispering, too. "Here?" I say.

"Yes, yes." He moves his hands impatiently. He looks over his shoulder. The woman at the front desk is looking at us. Above all, I don't want to make a spectacle. And Arthur looks very disturbed.

"Okay," I say, "okay, but quickly." Arthur steps back over to the woman at the desk. I go and stand by the elevators, out of sight of everything, dining room, front desk, stiff parlor chairs.

In a moment Arthur joins me. We get in the elevator, still behaving like strangers. I follow him down the hall. He has the key. He's walking quickly. He fumbles with the door. I begin to wonder why in the world we're doing this. I look behind us. The door opens with a cracking sound. We're in the room.

Arthur's moving very fast. Again he has that stricken look, as if something's wrong. He's taking off my clothes and his. I've never seen him like this. I don't even have time to think, to move. We're undressed. Daylight comes through the curtains. Out the window is a view of the school, the chapel, and the Green.

Arthur stops himself. "What am I doing?" he asks. "This could be terrible for you." He's staring at me. He looks like he might cry. After his habitual confidence, this look frightens me more than anything else.

"Don't worry," I say. "It doesn't matter."

I don't know what I'm saying and don't care. I just want him to stop looking at me like that. We go on, or he does. I hardly exist in this, or that's what it feels like. His eagerness frightens me. It's as if he can't control himself. I try to do something to regain myself, to feel something, but I can't. It's too much. His desire overwhelms me. It's like when you're knocked down and rolled by a wave. The shock and awkwardness of it, the discomfort, the sand and water in your ears and eyes and mouth. My eyes are looking out. I see the dull image of the blank TV staring back at me. I see the light fixture above, dull also, the light extinguished. There's no flaring, no flush, in me. It's as if I've been anesthetized, every part of me, head to toe. Does he notice this? Does he know? I can't tell. His wild look has disappeared. He's concentrating, private, his face lost in darkness. Then it's over, quickly, sharply.

"Oh, God," he says. He looks at me. "Was that okay?" He winces.

"Yes," I say. I nod. I keep my face smooth.

He puts his arms around me. He looks out the window and shakes his head, amazed. "I don't know what came over me," he says.

We lie there. He smooths my hair back with his hand. It feels nice, soothing. Or maybe it's just that I actually feel it, even if faintly, while I felt nothing that came before.

"We should go," he says.

I nod. I feel strangely impassive.

He leans up on his elbow. "How should we do this?" he asks.

I try to think of the situation, the fact that we're here at school. It's an effort. While it all seemed so important earlier, now it seems nearly meaningless. At last I manage something, a thought. "We shouldn't leave together," I say.

He gets up. "Do you want to go ahead?" he asks. "Why don't you go first?"

I lean up with effort on my elbows. "No, no, you go," I say. "It'll be better that way."

"Are you sure?"

"Yes, yes."

He's dressing, being practical again. "I'll pay downstairs," he says. "Wait ten minutes or so to be sure."

I nod. As he's covering himself up with his clothes, I see again, briefly, how beautiful he is. I'd forgotten. I smile.

"I'll call you," he says. He comes and kisses me, then disappears out the door.

I lie on the bed alone. The light outside the window seems to deepen. As I lie there, the gradual return of feeling creeps over me bit by bit, to and through each one of my limbs, my cheeks, my breasts and knees, the roots of my hair, my thighs, between each finger. I feel it happening. What was dead tingles, flushes. I feel like a plant that's being watered. I lie there quietly, letting it happen. At the same time, I begin to get a sense of the room, as if it, too, is coming alive, taking on a character and color, assuming a personality all its own. And like an air of music, a strain of a familiar melody returning, the memory of that other hotel room, the one in the city, comes back to me. Lying there, I begin to feel its raptures, not fully but dimly, like a song in the distance, muffled by the intervening air, still mixed with other sounds, faint and muffled, yet lovely all the same.

I'M IN MY ROOM STUDYING WHEN THE PHONE RINGS OUT IN the hall. I go to pick it up. It's Roe's voice, but it doesn't sound like her. She's choked up, crying.

"It's me, Roe," she says. Then she drops the phone. There's scrambling. The phone goes dead.

I rush back to my room and put on my shoes. Should I go out and find her? Should I wait? What if she calls again? I call her dorm. A girl answers. I say I want to speak to Roe. I hear the girl go and knock. She comes back. "She's not there."

"Are you sure?" I ask. "It's an emergency." My voice is shaking. "Will you open the door and look?"

The girl goes and comes back. "There's no one there," she says.

Roe must be with Jesse, either in his house or in that house in town.

I go outside. I want to run, but don't, so as not to draw attention. I hurry along, going the back way. I take the side street, where the friend's house is. As I turn down it, I see Roe's figure at the other end, running away.

"Roe!" I call. "Roe!" Roe looks back over her shoulder. She sees me, I'm sure of it, but keeps running. She must be running away from him, from that house. I glance in the house. The windows are empty. Then I see a flash of someone inside. It must be Jesse. I run after Roe. She's far ahead. When I get to the main street, she's nowhere in sight. She must have taken the back way, cutting through the trees.

I finally make it to her dorm. I rush up the stairs and knock on her door. It's locked. I call her name.

"Yes," she says, "I'm here. Something's happened," she says before she opens the door. I suck in my breath at the sight of her face. She's been beaten up. She has a broken lip and a swollen purple eye.

"He hit you?" I say. I can't grasp the thought. I'm not outraged, not anything. I'm trying to understand it.

"Yes," Roe says and bursts into tears. "I was running away," she says. "I saw you, but I had to run."

"That's fine, that's fine," I say.

She's locked the door behind me. The blinds are drawn. She's still crying but calms down slightly. I look at her face. "Shouldn't you do something?" I ask. "Shouldn't you put ice on it? I'll go get ice."

"No, don't leave," she says.

I stop. "Well, then I'll go tell someone to get ice. Ice, right? Isn't that what you're supposed to put on it?"

"Ask Anne," Roe says.

"Which one is she?"

Roe tells me which door to go to. I find Anne and ask her to get

some ice from the dining hall. "It's an emergency," I say, "for Roe."
She agrees.

When I come back, Roe is calmer. She looks at me as if realizing
for the first time what's happened. "I can't believe this," she says.

"Thank God you're all right, though," I say, "when I heard your
voice—"

"Yes, I know. It's that he came after me as I was on the phone."

"But why?"

She tells me what happened as well as she can. They were at the
friend's house. He'd had some whiskey. "He always makes up long,
elaborate lies," Roe says. "That's why I didn't believe him." He had
just told her that he'd been spying on her, almost since the beginning.
"He was saying it in a funny way. He was smiling in a way I didn't
understand. But then he started telling me about all these little things
I'd done alone at night in my room. Things I wouldn't have even
remembered or ever thought of, but there he was, telling me."

"Like what?"

"Well, like the way I'd tried on a shirt one night months ago."

"He was watching you."

"Yes, but more than that. He was watching from very close. He
knew what chapter I was reading in my history book the night
before last. So that means—"

"What?"

"That he was right outside, right outside my window on the fire
escape, sitting there looking in!"

"And what did you do when he told you this?"

"I was just so surprised by what he was saying. He even started
imitating me, things I'd done, the way I'd moved. Not in a mean

way, even tenderly. But I was so embarrassed, and I guess I felt betrayed. I just wanted to get away from him. So I started to leave. But he wouldn't let me. He blocked the door. When I tried to slip past, he lunged at me. He hit me once, hard, here on the mouth. I was shocked. I got up and got away from him. But he followed. I managed to lock myself in a room. That's when I called you. But then he broke through the door. He came after me and hit me again. I screamed. But then we heard someone pounding on the front door. It was a neighbor, I guess. Jesse went to talk to him. As they were talking, I snuck out the back door and ran. That's when I saw you, right after that."

Anne returns with the ice. I take it at the door. "Is Roe all right?" she asks.

"Yes, yes," I say. "She'll come by your room later."

Anne nods and leaves.

"I still can't believe it," Roe says. She's looking in the mirror at her face. She looks bewildered, frightened but also curious.

"Me, neither," I say.

I stay for a while. The blinds are pulled. We can't even see night fall.

"What will you tell people?" I ask.

Roe seems to have already worked this out. "That I tripped and fell down the stairs," she says.

JASPER CALLS AND LEAVES A MESSAGE, REPEATING HIS IN-vitation for me to spend the summer with him. I call Arthur im-mediately afterward to consolidate our plan. Then I write to my grandmother, saying I'm going to Europe on a summer trip with the school. She writes back that it's a marvelous idea and includes a check for what seems like an enormous sum.

The school year's ending. Roe and I take our exams, hand in our last papers. When I go over to see her, she's already begun packing, her bags out, in the middle of the floor. She's sitting by the window, wrapped in a flimsy blanket.

"How are you?" I ask.

She tries to smile. I've never seen her look like this. She has the blanket around her shoulders like an invalid, her hair down.

"Have you spoken to Jesse?" I ask.

"No. He's called a few times, but I haven't wanted to."

I sit down on the bed, too. We're both quiet.

"It's not only that he hit me. It's that I can't see him anymore," she says. She almost starts crying. "This is awful, isn't it? I didn't think it could be this awful. What has happened to us?" She drops her hands. "Look at me." She's half laughing, half crying. "Did we do something wrong?"

"I don't know," I say.

Roe wails, "I feel like I'll never feel normal again!"

I nod, though I don't feel despairing so much as more and more edgy. Roe was going to spend the summer with Jesse, or at least part of it, but now she's going home. I'm going with her to Georgia for two weeks, then coming back to meet Arthur in New York. The following day, we'll fly to France.

CHAPTER 10

ROE'S SHY WHEN INTRODUCING ME TO HER FATHER, PA, AND seems confused about how to behave. He's firmly built, muscular, with his hair cut short, as if he were still in the army. It's from him that Roe got her brown eyes and pale hair. But he won't acknowledge this. Later, he'll tell me, "Fortunately, the children got Linda's looks." ("He thinks he's very ugly," Roe explains.) He wears cowboy boots that might look absurd on someone else, but they don't on him.

Roe's father looks as though he's prepared at any moment to fend off life in case it should attack. He has the blow ready to defend himself and his family. This is the impression he gives, that he would die in a second for Roe. I glance over at her. It has always seemed to me that she has in her something I don't, a certain solidity, as if she might have known from the start, suspected all along, who she was.

Her father's tenderness is very gruff, very distant. He does all the household work. Once Roe's mother died, he started to do it himself, meticulously. He sweeps the floor every day. "They learn how to in the army," Roe says. "He never lets a day go by without cleaning."

Her father is on his way to work when Roe and I arrive. He runs a small fast-food restaurant. He's not at all talkative, not, it seems, very comfortable with people.

"Sometimes he relaxes," Roe says, "in the evenings at the restaurant, when he's sitting with his friends having a beer. But during the day, he's nearly always like that."

I laugh, not at what she's saying but at her accent. It's already grown more pronounced. "Your accent," I say.

"I know," Roe answers, covering her mouth with one hand.

Roe and I walk through the town. It's small and dusty. There are few streets. Some aren't even paved. The hot air lilts ever so slightly; you can hear all around the whirring of fans. "Next you'll meet my brother," Roe says. She rolls her eyes. "And then you'll really wonder about me."

The town has just two sites. One is the thrift store, the other the Bluebird Café. We go to the thrift store first. It's a charity organization run by one family. Roe went to school with the daughter and son. She's come here for years to get her clothes.

"You always were a character," the mother says to Roe. She turns to the woman beside her. "Do you remember how she used to buy those men's pants?"

"Shh! She's still wearing them," the other woman says.

Roe laughs. We look around briefly. "We'll be back," Roe says. We go on to the Bluebird Café.

"Nice, isn't it?" Roe asks once we've stepped inside. It used to be an old factory building. The ceilings are high, with pipes across them. Below are small tables with blue tops, a counter with plates of homemade cookies and brownies. Roe knows the girl who comes to wait on us. She's older than Roe, went to her old school. But Roe's become a bit of a celebrity now that she's gone away.

"You're back!" the girl says.

"She never used to give me the time of day," Roe tells me once the girl's gone.

It's not yet noon. The day is getting hotter. The heat gathers glaringly out in the streets while, inside, the fans whir on. Roe stares out the window. This is where she'll spend the summer. I'm going on my trip.

"You see what I mean?" she says. "There's nothing, nothing, nothing to do!"

"If only you could come with me," I say. Then I qualify this because, said that way, it might sound false. "I mean, assuming of course that I wasn't going with Arthur."

"And that I even could," Roe says. She has no money and no possible source of money unless she makes it herself. She looks around her. "Maybe I can get a job here." She used to work at the Five-and-Dime.

The girl has left, and now there's a boy behind the counter, the owner's son, Roe thinks. Roe signals to him. "I'm interested in getting work here," she says. "Do you have any openings?"

The boy brings Roe an application. We look at it together. "Education, previous experience." Roe fills it out.

"So that's something," she says, "if I get this job. Otherwise I'll read. I'll read and read and read."

I think of it, the hot days, the fans whirring, sitting back and reading. It sounds so appealing, and like a relief compared to what I'm poised to do. "It sounds nice to me right now if I think of it," I say.

Roe leans forward on her arms. "Really? But the days go so slowly. You have no idea how slowly the days go."

She takes me to the quarry outside of town. The quarry water is deep, black-green. There's a raft you can lie out on. Roe wears an old bathing suit of her mother's, a one-piece, dark and loose. We lie out in the sun. Above is the quarry cliff, its reflection looming over the water. The rest of the shore is hung thick with trees, the trees themselves hung thick with broad-leaved vines.

We lie on the raft until we're hot, then dive in. The upper layer of the water is warm from the sun, but deeper down it jolts you, it's so cold. Sometimes we stay in for a little while, treading water, or we swim to the base of the cliff and back. But mostly we loll on the raft.

We've hardly talked about my trip. I prefer not to. The idea of it, for some reason, makes me uneasy. I want to lie there and not think about it. Just for the moment, just for now. As for Roe's boy, we also hardly mention him. Two days pass without a word. Then, on the third, as we're lying on the raft, his name appears. She mentions him in passing, something he said. Although we talked about it after it happened, she tells me again how they said good-bye.

She saw him one night standing outside her dorm. By chance, she'd happened to look out her window. He was there, standing very still in the trees. She watched for a moment, then pulled down the blind. But the following day, when he called, she agreed to talk. And the day after that, she went to meet him in town. They had coffee in the diner. He'd left her alone all this time. Her eye was completely healed. They talked for a little while, then kissed.

Roe looks down as she tells me this. She's embarrassed. "I felt like it."

"Don't be embarrassed with me," I say.

"I shouldn't be, should I?"

"No, of course not."

"Well then, yes, we kissed. I felt like it, so I did. I knew I wouldn't see him for a long time."

Her head is lifted. She's on her elbows. My face is flattened against the raft. I raise it to speak. "How did you leave it?" I ask.

"We said we'd see each other in September, when I got back to school. I said I didn't think we should meet sooner. I'm pretty sure he would have liked to do something this summer. That had been our plan. But after I said that, he was very casual. I think he was actually mad. He said, 'Yeah, sure, if I'm still around.'"

"What did he mean?"

"That he might be leaving. He said he wants to take off on his own."

"Without finishing school?"

"He doesn't care about school."

"Does he know where to find you?"

"He has the address. I gave it to him in case he wanted to write, but he won't."

"Do you mind not seeing him?"

"No," Roe says. She looks down, then over at me. It's an edgy look. She drops her eyes again. "I only wish what happened hadn't happened."

I turn over, facing up toward the sun.

"Do you ever feel like an impostor?" I ask after a little while.

She looks at me, puzzled.

"With him, I mean," I say. "As if you were pretending to be someone you're not?"

She thinks. "No," she says, "not really." She pauses, then goes on, picking her way. "What I *do* feel is that he doesn't really know me."

"Me, too," I say. "I feel as though Arthur hardly knows me at all. I actually think he thinks I'm someone else entirely, and—" I stop short.

"What?"

"Well." I sit up, uncomfortably. I'm feeling more and more worried. "I just wonder what will happen if he finds me out."

Roe looks at me, her expression serious. "Maybe you shouldn't go."

I think of Jasper's letter, and of going home. "No, no, I have to."

"You could stay here," she says.

For a moment the possibility hangs there, suspended. Then it passes.

Roe introduces me to her friend Laura. We go over to her house. Laura's waiting for us out in the yard. She's tiny, with short jet-black hair. She looks like a little bird, a crow, and has Roe's accent but stronger.

"Let's go," Laura says as soon as we arrive. We can see the figure of her mother moving around inside. We start walking down the sidewalk. Laura's in the middle, smaller than both of us. "I just can't stand to be in that house anymore."

She takes us to meet her girlfriend, Tina. She's excited for Roe to meet her. Tina's doing landscaping around the school. As we walk, we try to stick to the shade. The leaves on the trees are dusty. Out in the street the sun glares down.

"This is Tina Wiles, right, Brian's older sister?" Roe asks Laura.

"Uh-huh. She went away. But then came back a year ago," Laura says. "She's older, twenty-six."

We arrive at the school. There's a chain-link fence around it. Laura calls out. Tina's bending down, wearing rubber gloves, as she clears bushes away. She straightens, then walks over to us at the fence. She wears a T-shirt and pants, is strong, short-haired, her expression sheltered, wary. But she's clearly very happy to see Laura. She barely looks at Roe and me, has to force herself to. She and Laura grip fingers through the fence.

That night we all go to a tractor pull, Roe and I with Laura and Tina and a few other friends of theirs. The cars are jacked up. They have their mufflers off. The stadium lights are bright, the air full of incredible noise. We get a lottery number with our tickets on the way in. They're selling beer and boiled peanuts in the stands. We have to shout above the noise.

Roe shouts something I can't understand, her accent so strong that we both start laughing. Halfway through the races, a lottery number is called. It's Roe's. Roe shows Laura. Laura jumps up.

"You've won!" she says. "Go down there. You've just won a car!"

Roe pulls my sleeve. "Come with me," she says. We walk down the stadium steps. Roe shows her ticket and they let us onto the track. The man below asks Roe her name, then says it into the microphone. He lifts her hand high in the air. Roe flushes. The whole stadium cheers. We get into the car, Roe driving. The motor roars. The car bounces as if on giant bed springs. We drive off the track and park in the parking lot.

That night, we drive the car home. It's late. The houses in Roe's neighborhood are all dark. Roe's street is quiet. The car along it makes a terrible tearing sound. Roe and I wince. We pull up in front of her house. The sound is deafening. Roe turns the car off. We sit inside for a moment; Roe's waiting to see what will happen. Her father's light goes on.

"Oh no," Roe says. "Don't move."

Her father comes out the front door in his pajamas. "Who the hell is that?" he says. His voice is menacing. He has a gun.

"It's me, Pa. Roe."

Her father lowers the gun. "What the hell are you doing?" Now that he sees it's her, he's furious. This is the kind of misbehavior he can't abide. "Where did you get that thing?"

"Sorry, Pa," Roe says through the open slit of her window.

"Don't tell me sorry. Tell me what the hell you're doing."

"I won this at the track," Roe says. "I didn't know what to do with it."

"I'll tell you what to do with it. You take it away from here."

"Now?"

"No, not now. Now you get in the house."

Roe and I gingerly open the car doors. We shut them as quietly as we can, then walk past her father, still holding his gun.

Roe's brother and his wife come to dinner. They're born-again Christians, both twenty-two. They already have two children. Roe's brother looks like her physically, but their attitude and behavior are so different, the mobility, the light in the face and eyes. Maybe if they were sleeping side by side, the resemblance would be clear, but as it is, it comes in flashes, the occasional identical gesture, the movement of a hand. As night falls, the air cools. We sit outside in the back, where Roe's father cooks a barbecue. The yard is small but cropped and clean. Wisteria climbs up the back of the house. Roe's father doesn't say much as he cooks the food. He stands to one side. But he listens.

Roe and I talk to her brother and his wife. They're very friendly. We play with the kids. Over dinner, they begin talking about something that happened in town. A man was killed. It was an accident, apparently. Someone's gun went off. The Miller boys were involved. Roe and I are asking all kinds of questions. Roe's brother and his wife know the details. Roe's father doesn't say much. He purses his lips, walks back over to the grill, flips the last hamburger.

After dinner, we all sit back in our chairs. The light is fading. Fireflies are beginning to rise from the grass. The kids chase after them. Roe's brother's wife is talking about a movie that just came out. She really wanted to see it. She likes the actor. Only then someone told her that he plays a gay guy. She starts laughing. "And I said, 'No, thank you,'" she says, "'I think I'll miss that one.'"

"Why?" Roe asks, putting the question very directly, very innocently.

The wife smiles, surprised, then looks over at Roe's brother and shuts up.

"If it's something that exists?" Roe goes on.

There's a silence. Her brother, Tommy, looks perplexed, as if he'd rather not get involved.

"Because it isn't right," Roe's father says, getting up again. "I know it exists, but it isn't right. You do those things in private."

"Why?" Roe asks.

Roe's father's back is turned. He begins fiddling with the grill, scraping it off. "Because those things should be private," he says. "Otherwise you'll give other young people ideas."

"It says in the Bible that it isn't right," Tommy says, clearing his throat.

Roe whips her face around. "Oh, please, Tommy! Stop it!"

"Now, that's enough," their father says.

"Enough of what?" Roe asks.

"Of this talk."

"No, Pa, I'm not finished."

"Roe, I'm warning you."

"Well, I'm warning *you*. I'm not finished."

"Is this what I sent you away to school for? So you can act like this?" her father asks.

But Roe won't stop. Her father, so as not to do anything else, it seems, walks across the yard. Roe goes after him.

"Roe, don't do that," Tommy says.

"Why? Why not? Why can't I say what I think?" She keeps following her father, then turns back to look at Tommy. "Remember Laura? Well, she's gay."

"I know that," Tommy says. "I live here, Roe. Everyone knows it, everyone sees it."

"And so?"

Roe runs after her father. He's gone out the back gate. There's the sound of a truck starting, then Roe yelling. There's no answer from her father. The truck drives away. Roe comes back into the yard, crying in frustration and rage. Tommy goes toward her, hugs her. She lets him for an instant, then breaks away. She runs toward the house, going in the back door. I follow, catching up with her on the sidewalk out front.

We walk.

"What's the point?" Roe asks after a little while. "What do you actually want?" Then she answers herself. "You just want someone to listen, to actually listen to you. Not someone, them! You want them to actually listen just once." The thought of it makes her furious again. "I've seen that so often, his back walking away. I could just put a knife in it." She calms down a little, keeps walking. "Why have they never tried to understand anything about me?"

CHAPTER 11

ON THE PLANE TO PARIS, I LOOK OUT THE WINDOW. ARTHUR, head turned, is asleep beside me. Clouds, only clouds. I watch them. I imagine falling, falling through those clouds. At first it just seems like a dreamy thought, but then I can't stop picturing it, leaping out, falling. What is happening? I feel dizzy. I close my eyes. But even without looking, I keep seeing myself falling, jumping and falling. The glare of the light comes through my eyelids. It's there outside the window, the dizzying fall. I pull the blind down, turn away. Across the aisle, I see a red light by the emergency-exit door. It suddenly occurs to me—that's where I'll jump. No, no, don't think it, but I can't stop. My heart is beating rapidly now, high up in my chest. It feels like it's in my throat. I move to stand. I'm jerked back by the seat belt. I try to undo it but can't. I'm stuck. My heart is beating uncontrollably. I try to breathe but can't, or can just barely. My chest is so tight, so shallow, there's no space for the air. I take short, shallow breaths. I yank at the seat belt, break free.

I stand. I'm on my feet now, but where will I go? Arthur turns in his sleep. Please no, don't wake now. The idea of confronting him in this state is too much. I step over his legs and am out in the aisle. My heart is pounding, my breath quick and shallow. I look around wildly. Where will I go? A stewardess comes by. She says something, I don't hear what exactly. I nod but can't speak. My throat's shut entirely. I can't even swallow. Spit is building up in my mouth. I see the emergency door again. I have to get out of this plane. Am I heading toward it? I force myself to turn, to go the other way, down the corridor to the bathroom.

I go into the bathroom, close the door, and lock it. I sit down, put my head down, but my mind won't stop. I see myself again and again, flinging open the emergency door. And then what? Jumping, throwing myself out. The air blowing in, the wind, the whole sky. Mayhem, everything swirling. Would everyone else be pulled out, too? If I did this, would all of us die? Or be crushed by the pressure? Where did I get that idea? I imagine people collapsing, their chests caving in.

I can still hardly breathe. I'm sitting, leaning over, my heart beating madly. Spit is drooling out the sides of my mouth. There's even less air in the bathroom than outside. But I don't dare go out, pass by that door again.

They say the body can sustain only a certain amount of panic. When a limit is reached, it emits a drug—that must be what's happening. I don't know how much time has passed, but suddenly I feel it, like a deliverance, coursing through my limbs. My heart slows, I go weak, I can swallow. After a few minutes, I return to my seat. Once there, I fall back, let my arms sink. I lie there, feeling this substance spread through me. My chest releases, my heart sinks. There's space in my lungs. Air can enter. I breathe and drop my head back, closing my eyes.

When I wake, Arthur smiles at me. He takes my hand. Before, we were flying over ocean, only ocean. Now we see a spit of land, a brown edge filled with green, and then a long rim, a coast. The sun beams down on it.

PARIS. THE KNOT OF STREETS. THE NARROW CURVED SIDE-walks along which you walk, sometimes nearly pressed against the wall. The red awnings, the red cafés, the corner cafés in which you sit, tight and squeezed at tiny tables, the spreading cafés, the sprawling ones with mirrored walls, the famous ones with upstairs rooms with windows, out of which your gaze falls down to the streets, the cafés with outside tables, the ones with straw chairs whose dominant color is green not red, the cafés that are always copied, the red and gold ones.

The sudden emergence after the narrow streets into a square, sometimes large and lovely and solemn, lined with trees; or else small and hidden, hardly a square, a grayed statue in the center, the lichen on the stones black and green. The river, the water rippling almost foolishly, the leaves on the trees along it flapping in the wind, flipping up their silver undersides. The quay, built of shifting, sinking stone, its round contours, its pickup spots, dark designated areas, the benches out in the open, the sunbathers, the boats churning by. At night the boats throw up their lights on the buildings, on the upper windows of the sinking buildings, on the trees, blanching all their leaves.

The swooping curve of the bridges, navigating the islands, the avenues, the parks. The rue des Écoles, tripping happily along the edge of the hill. The hill itself climbs, it mounts and mounts, weighted down with heavy buildings, you trip up goatlike, the dark prisonlike buildings or the smooth sand-colored ones pressing down on each side.

We go to the Louvre. Arthur's excitement is that of a child. We look at statues. There's a young girl running.

"She looks like you," Arthur says.

"Like me?" I ask.

In the Rodin museum, the figures shine as if by moonlight. The Centre Pompidou has whole walls of glass. As we're going up in the elevator, I feel woozy. It seems I'm terrified of heights. It's not that I'll fall but that I'm afraid I'll jump.

I picture myself jumping, everywhere we go. Off rooftops, out of windows, off bridges and quays into the water, off buses, out of taxi doors. I picture myself in the subway leaping in front of trains. I stand back near the subway walls. If I feel really tempted, I grip on to something, a post or a chair.

"What are you doing?" Arthur asks.

"Nothing."

He looks at me, puzzled. I quickly look away. I can even feel myself falling when there's nowhere to fall to, when I'm sitting on a bench.

We walk along the quay, arm in arm. We pass under bridges. The smell of urine is intoxicating. It overwhelms you, makes you want to fall backward. We go on. Another bridge. There are men loitering, looking at each other.

As we're walking along the streets, stone faces peer down at us, carved into the buildings, some childlike, cherublike; some horrific, gargoyles with their lips unfurled. That's how all faces look, I think, when you're afraid. I'm afraid, but of what? I clutch Arthur's arm as we're walking, but I don't dare look at him.

We go to the street where Arthur's family lived when he was a child. He finds the building. "There, the third floor," he says. We look up at the windows. They open outward, like most Paris windows. They're hung with lace curtains.

I stare up. I can't imagine this at all, Arthur, a boy, living here, stepping out to school. He, on the other hand, seems to see it vividly. He's strangely refreshed. He can't believe he hasn't been back here for over fifteen years. What was he thinking?

I nod. I feel lost inside myself, shut up inside. It's as if I'm wandering inside a dark house. The windows are bolted, the doors all closed.

"Are you all right?" he asks. "What's wrong?"

"Nothing, nothing."

The hotels we stay in are dark, carpeted monochrome places, tiny. We change from one to the next. Finally we find a nicer one near the university. It looks out on a square where students gather. They seem my age or a little older. It occurs to me one day as I'm watching them that that's all over, it's already too late for me. I'll never gather like that in a square.

Arthur tells me I seem different.

"In what way?"

"I don't know. Even the way you move."

"How do I move?"

"Well, I don't know, but you used to have a kind of grace. Not a ballerina-grace but another kind of individual—I don't know how else to put it—grace."

That's what's lacking, grace. But maybe I can retrieve it. Maybe it's not entirely gone. Lift the arm, hold the neck. I've let my muscles grow weak. Exercise, air. That's what I need. Maybe it all boils down to that, stepping out, as they say, and "taking some air."

Arthur goes out for the day. He has research to do, buildings to look at. I go out a bit later on my own—I force myself. The university, as I pass, fills me with wonder. I peek in the courtyard.

"Let's go in," Arthur says, appearing at my elbow, out of nowhere.

I look at him, frightened. I feel as though I must have done something wrong. More and more, I have the feeling that I'll be apprehended and even arrested for doing things wrong.

"I just wanted to go out," I say, "to get some air."

He gives me a funny look. "Yes, yes, that's fine."

Everything I do seems suspicious. I feel as though I even look suspicious, as if, when I'm walking down the street, I'm hunching over, my legs bent, listing slightly sideways. I'm sure I'll be stopped, thrown up against a wall, and that I'll deserve it, though I won't know why. Any kind of official character in uniform, a doorman, a policeman, a guard, fills me with unreasonable fear. My knees lock as I pass them. I lurch forward. That I manage to stay upright at all seems like a miraculous feat.

If you think too much about anything, it becomes impossible. If you fear that your body won't be able to perform all the natural processes we do by rote—walking, breathing, swallowing—and you try to do them consciously, to force yourself to breathe, to walk (walking is so complicated), then it's impossible. The system lurches, jars. The strain is immense, the movements all unnatural, things grind to a halt.

"Should we go in?" Arthur asks.

I glance at the guard by the university gate. Will he let us pass? I'm holding Arthur's arm, but I'm on the side near the guard. No, no, I should be on the other side, where he can't see me. I force myself to take a step, then another, cringing away from the guard as we pass.

We enter the courtyard of the university, the rough pale stones underfoot. To one side is the chapel, and to the other, arcades with lamps hanging from their ceilings. We turn and look up at the windows. I imagine chairs being hurled from these windows in student protests. I picture a chair being hurled down on us right now. Along the other edge of the courtyard is a row of glass doors. Someone comes out, a girl student, her hair up. Arthur looks at her. I do, too. She stops in the courtyard to light a cigarette. Arthur smiles. We admire her.

"Come," Arthur says, taking my elbow, "let's look inside."

He's picked up the habit of holding my elbow when we walk, as if I'm an old woman or an invalid. It's happened without discussion. I must have indicated without speaking my weakness, my fear of falling. But that's only part of it. He doesn't know the rest, how I'm becoming decrepit in other ways, my faculties failing little by little. It's harder to see, to hear. Nothing sticks in my mind, the names of people, places. It all ripples through. My mind is like a sieve.

We cross the courtyard and go through one of the swinging glass doors. Arthur holds it open for me. In the hallway, students mill around, looking at papers tacked to a board. There's another set of doors. Arthur peers in. He motions for me to come. There's an enormous room inside, an amphitheater, its seats and walls made of wood. Arthur points to the ceiling.

"Look."

There are paintings, large murals, high up on the walls. Of what? I can't see exactly. Huge beings, goddesses. One with a harp stands facing the others, a child angel beside her. The meadow around them is wondrously green. Looking up, I feel again that fear of falling. It's a rush. I keep looking. I almost wouldn't mind, I think, falling this way, up into that meadow.

"Come on," Arthur says. He takes my elbow. He wants to look around. I want to stay here, gazing up at that meadow, but I follow him. We walk down the wide polished halls, up and down steps, along smaller corridors, through different doors. I watch the students in their dark clothes, coming in and out of doorways, walking along corridors, sitting on benches. Their books, cigarettes, pale faces, laughter. I envy them. But from far, very far. They seem to me worlds away.

We walk along the quays, back to the quays. The leaves trembling in the light.

We go to the parks, they confuse me, the way everything is laid out so perfectly. In the Tuilerie Gardens, we pass plots of flowers, then enter an area dark and cool with tree shade. There's the ornate part, the statues, the large glassy fountain, the chairs set around it in a circle.

I look at the fountain, the stretches of gravel and tree shade behind it. "What's wrong with you? Does nothing please you?" the voice in my head asks. Yes, certain things do. Like those shadows of tree shade behind the fountain.

It's as if my mind is clouded over, but there's one layer that's luminous and clear. This is where I see things, the things that please me. Only I can't see them when Arthur's near. It's as if the force of him paralyzes me. My mind clouds over. It's not his fault, or is it? No, there's something wrong with me. When I'm alone, the light flickers again, things reappear.

We sit down by the fountain in the sun. Maybe this is what I need, I think, days and days of this, sitting here without moving in the sun. But not with Arthur. I know that much. I can't recuperate with him here. It strikes me that I'll never get better as long as he's here. Then I forget that thought. I really do feel better today, I tell myself. Maybe I'm just tired, it's sure to pass.

He's talking about his childhood again. He's thinking of it almost constantly. Everything, all of it, is reviving in him slowly. He feels it, he says, he can even see it, like a dark place that's being infused with light. He remembers coming to this fountain, for example, playing here with his brother. "It's as if I remembered nothing," he says, "and suddenly it's all here." He even looks younger, his face flushed with light.

I nod. Or at least I try to, but my neck is stiff.

"What is it? What's wrong?" He's exasperated. That's clear now. It sounds in his voice.

"Nothing, nothing."

We get up and walk on. "Are you hungry?" he asks. I don't know, I can't tell what I am anymore, hungry, tired. I keep my head ducked almost constantly. I'm not sleeping well. I'm more and more afraid of being with him, face-to-face, I'm above all afraid of having nothing to say.

We go to a restaurant. We sit opposite each other. The waiter's jocular in an annoying way. He's surely making fun of us, or at least of me.

I wait until Arthur orders. Even if it's something I don't like—

lamb—I say very quickly, "The same," to avoid speaking more than two words.

"I thought you didn't like lamb," Arthur says.

I shrug. "No, I do."

He seems irritated. He doesn't like the way I begin all my sentences with "no."

"Sorry," I say.

"For what?"

"For saying 'no.'"

He doesn't understand what I mean. I try to think of something else to say. The best would be something casual. Or better still, something funny. I try to remember if I ever said something funny before. I used to be able to make Roe laugh. Once she even laughed so hard, she felt sick. Maybe I should tell Arthur this.

"I once made Roe laugh so hard she felt sick," I say.

Arthur looks at me, surprised. "Really? You did?"

"Yes," I say, looking down, ashamed to have said such a pathetic thing.

If only a storm would come, a fire, something tragic, so that in a moment we would all be swept away. I picture being swept away from Arthur, or on second thought, I see myself being very brave amid a disaster. We'd be up in the air, but I'd grip his sleeve. All around us would be flying rocks and metal beams. But would I really be so brave? The truth is, I'm not so sure.

But a disaster in any case would be nice. Afterward, in the wreckage, we could begin all over again. In the wreckage, imagine how relieved we'd feel. How many new things we'd have to say. I'd say, "Remember when that beam flew so close to your head? Did you see

that woman's face? I wonder what happened to that little brown dog."
He'd say, "You held on to me so tightly." "If it hadn't been for you,"
we'd say, "how terrible"—"the noise"—"and the fire!" "Yes, the fire!"

"What are you thinking?" Arthur asks.

I freeze when he says this. That is, I'm already still, but I feel my
insides freeze.

"Nothing," I say.

This irritates him, too.

"No, I just thought it might be nice—if there were a disaster, I
mean right now—not an accident, with people killed, necessarily,
but, I mean, a terrible disaster, anyway, of some kind."

"Wonderful," he says, "just what we need."

The waiter passes, moving fast. "Could we—" I say to him, "that
is, could I—please have some wine?"

The waiter turns volte-face and rattles off a long list of wines. I
can't hear what he's saying or distinguish the sounds.

"Yes," I say, confused.

"Yes what?" he asks. He turns and winks at Arthur.

"Whatever you think," I say, more confused.

"You should be careful," Arthur says once the waiter's gone.
"You really do drink a lot. I have nothing against it. But it's something to watch out for, that's all. Just to keep a hand in. It's good every
once in a while to just say, 'Tonight I won't drink.' "

All right, I think, tonight I won't. I'll tell the waiter to take the
wine back. I fumble for some bread. The little basket falls. Crumbs
everywhere.

In the mornings, Arthur goes out while I stay in the room. Lying
there, I recover a slight feeling, a trace of a memory of that other

hotel room, the one in New York where I stayed alone. It appears like the first notes of a song, then fades. I lie there very still, but it doesn't come back. It's that his presence annuls; even when he's gone, there's the presence of his things. It's a force that overwhelms any force I might have. I'm left one corner, a small patch of floor.

I begin to feel nostalgic for myself and the way I used to be. Suddenly, I realize that I've lost the walk. I can feel it. I've lost the walk. I had it before without even knowing it. Maybe, I think, I can get it back. Maybe I should practice walking back and forth across the room. But I can only do this when Arthur's gone.

I wait for the moments when he's gone. If only because then my chest feels less tight. I imagine how I'll be when he returns. I try to prepare myself by lying very quietly. Better still is to take a hot bath.

How I'll be: light-stepped, freshly washed. Glancing out the window impatiently. Dashing to the mirror to fix my hair. There's music. Is it me? Am I singing? Yes, that's it. To be singing quite unconsciously this or that song. What song? I don't know any songs. All I can think of is that one about the war: "Where Have All the Flowers Gone?" That will never do. But there are millions of songs. Although I rarely listen to music—and suspect, to be honest, that I have a dead ear—I must be able to come up with at least one appropriate song.

Too late. He's at the door.

My throat is tight. I have a cough. When we try to have sex, I cough and expel him.

Alone in the room one day, I feel restless. I want to go out, too, at least to get a cup of coffee. I'm still in my nightgown. I peer out the window. Could I? Step out on my own and get a cup of coffee? It seems inconceivable. Then I think of the way I used to take the bus alone, arrive in the city alone. But I feel confused. Could that really have been me? I go to the mirror and look at myself. I see signs of age all over my face. How did it happen? I see dark circles, lines. Has Arthur not noticed this? He must have, surely, but hasn't said anything. It's because he feels sorry for me, I think.

The thought of going out for a cup of coffee falls by the wayside. What's wrong with me? I keep returning to the mirror. My face looks ravaged. I wash it; it looks worse, the skin red now, the circles deeper. I exhaust myself. Finally I lie down. I see myself again stepping out for a drink alone in the city. Again I think it—could that really have been me? How carelessly I did it, how I looked up, not down, seeing everything. Surely I can step out now, however briefly.

I get up and put on a dress. It's the wrong one. It feels scratchy, silly. I look in the mirror. Everyone will laugh at me with this thing on. I choose another. It looks even worse, even stranger. What could I have been thinking, wearing these dresses? I'm beginning to feel clammy. There's no air in the room. How am I to go out if I can't wear any of these things? Glancing around, I see Arthur's clothes. Maybe I can wear something of his. He's put his clothes away neatly, hung in the closet, folded in the drawers. I try on a shirt, then some pants. Everything's too big, but I tuck the shirt into the pants, then put on a belt and tighten it. I look in the mirror again. This looks a bit strange, but better than the dresses.

I find some money Arthur has left out on the bureau. And the key, I'll need the key. I'll leave it at the desk downstairs. But I doubt absolutely everything. Is that what you're supposed to do in hotels? I think of the woman and man who work there. If I hand them the key, will they look at each other and laugh?

I walk down the stairs in Arthur's clothes. I pass the front desk and slip the key onto it. I already feel like hiding. If only a wall would close up behind me, leaving not the slightest mark. I make it out the door and into the square. The light and air are overwhelming. The students are gathered. I stay clear of them, walking near the walls, my shoulders grazing corners. It feels safer this way. I glance at one café, am about to enter, then hesitate, too late, I have to go on now. I peer in another. No, the waiter looked at me, I've already made a spectacle. I go on. I pass a shop for clothes. Maybe I should try to buy some. Someone's entering behind me, a woman with a baby. Because of her forward movement, I'm forced to step inside. The girl working there looks up at me. I look away. She says something. I have no idea what. I shake my head and turn to leave. I run into a student carrying a backpack on her way in.

"Sorry," I say, reeling slightly from the blow, then barging out past her. Crazy, what was I thinking, going in there. To think this is the moment to buy clothes. No, the thing to do is find a café. I'm out on the street again. They're everywhere, the cafés. It's impossible to choose. Worse still, to have to go inside, to be stared at, to sit and ask for something. I keep starting to go in, then hesitating. Once I hesitate, I can't.

By now I've come to the edge of a park. A spiked iron fence encloses it. LUXEMBOURG GARDENS, a sign says. Maybe it would be easier to take a walk in the park. Then I don't have to sit, to say anything. I walk along trying to find an opening in the fence. Yes, the park is definitely better. Then everyone won't be staring. There'll be bushes and trees. I find the gate and go inside. There are paths under trees, and out in the open, neat plots of flowers. Except for a small rectangular spot that seems to be designated for children, there are no people on the grass. The grass rises up, perfectly cut and combed. Then I come to some white marble steps. Below is a dazzling scene. This is what is meant by the Luxembourg Gardens. There's an immense white fountain, around it a glimmering extensive pool, and around that, like in the Tuileries, chairs set in a grand circle and people sitting out in the sun, talking or reading. They have their legs crossed. Some smoke. A few have their legs up on another chair.

I remember how I thought about recuperating by a fountain, sitting there day after day in the sun. This is what I'll do, I think. I'll sit down here, put my head back. The sun seeps into me. I close my eyes. I haven't slept well for nights and nights, an hour or so here and there, and then an hour or so in the mornings once Arthur's gone. I can't sleep well with him near. Now I do. I finally sleep hard, plunging downward.

After what seems to be hours, I emerge. I pull myself up, stiff from the chair. For a moment, I can't imagine where I am or why I'm wearing these clothes. I look at the water in the fountain. Then I remember gradually, Paris. And Arthur. And my escape from the hotel room.

I feel rested but weak. I still haven't eaten or drunk anything. I stand up and look around, then walk up the marble steps and, still inside the park, come upon something that looks like a café. People are sitting at tables under trees. I sit down, too. The waiter comes over. He's quick and impatient. I order a coffee and a sandwich with cheese. It's not really what I want, but they're the only French words

I come up with. The sandwich tastes delicious when it comes. It has butter in it.

I've gotten away, but at some point I'll need to go back. Won't I? But how? I've completely lost my bearings. And what if I never do? I have nothing with me. I check my pockets. I have some change but not my bank card. No, I absolutely must find my way back.

I look for the waiter. My movements, each one, must be planned in advance. I ask the waiter for the bill and some water. I take a sip of water, pay, and make my move. First I need to get out of the park. I leave the café and walk until I find the entrance gate. I step out. But I can't remember the name of the street the hotel is on. I can't remember the name of the hotel. All I remember is the square full of students. I need to find this square. It's in the neighborhood of the university. I begin walking. Café after café after café. They all look familiar, but I can't be sure. Then I get to a larger street that I know is not familiar. I walk on, now and then taking a turn. But these turns seem to be leading me farther and farther away. I'm getting more and more lost. Now I've even lost sight of the park.

Arthur will be mad at me, I'm sure. I nearly always see him now in this posture of anger or irritation. It's the gargoyle face. I see it everywhere.

I go into a café and head for the bathroom. The waiter says something to me. What? It could be anything, but I'm sure he's telling me to get out. I turn around and leave. I try another. This waiter shakes his head and says something. I turn again and leave. Back on the street, I keep walking. I really need to go to the bathroom. I see a sign for what looks like a public bathroom. It's down some stone steps. I go down. The smell is overwhelming. There's a hallway and a door marked WOMEN and one marked MEN. I go into the women's bathroom. It's filthy. I go to the bathroom as quickly as I can without touching anything. As I'm coming out and heading up the stairs, I see a man coming down slowly. He sees me, too. He's wearing an overcoat. He pauses on the stairs and opens the coat, his eyes on me. His pants are open. I can see everything. It looks like a blooming white flower. My heart seizes. I want to back away. But I keep moving past him up the stairs. Up on the street, I walk away fast, my heart pounding with each step. Now what? Now I really do want to get back.

I stop in a café for shelter. For a moment, I feel safer with other people near. Then I go out again. I turn and turn and turn. The streets start to grow dark. I'm beginning to panic. I forget about the way a city lights itself and imagine that it will soon be pitch dark, night, nothing. I imagine running into the walls of the stone buildings, scraping my face, breaking off teeth. All at once, after another turn, I come upon a building that looks like the university, not the side I know but maybe the back. I walk around it. It's immense, the infinite walls rising. I even begin to feel that I must be mistaken. Then I see it at last, down a narrow street, a glimmer of the square of students. I walk toward the square. The last students are departing. I see our hotel, slow down. After all that, I almost don't want to go in.

I climb the stairs.

"There you are," Arthur says. "Where were you?"

"Out. I went for a walk."

He looks at my clothes and smiles. "What are you wearing?" he asks.

"Oh," I say, afraid he'll be mad, "your clothes."

"It's all right," he says. "My God." He must have seen my expression, the fear in my face.

"Sorry," I say.

"Stop!" he says. "Stop saying you're sorry."

I'm about to say it again. I hold my lips tight together so I won't.

CHAPTER 12

WE'RE IN THE TRAIN STATION. ARTHUR CARRIES THE BAGS. I stand there useless, or I struggle behind him. I feel as if I'm always lagging behind him. Is this because he walks fast, or because I prefer it, not to have to walk side by side? He shoots me back an irritated glance.

"Come on!" he says.

I try to catch up, though I don't want to. I want to be alone, if only because then I can breathe, but I'm scared on the other hand to go out alone. More and more, I feel that I can do nothing on my own. My arms and legs, my fingers and feet, seem to have lost their dexterity. Although I've studied French in school, I can't remember anything.

"But I thought you knew some French," Arthur says.

It's true. I even remember reading several books in French, short ones that were easy to read, like *L'Étranger* by Camus. Now that seems impossible. I picture the wake following the Paris boats, the thick lines of foam, how they sink and fade. By the end nothing's left. All of it gone.

I can no longer hear well. Everything's muffled, faraway. But the thing that bothers Arthur most is that when I speak, my voice barely appears. It's lost somewhere, wandering, inside my throat.

Arthur goes off to buy the tickets, leaving me alone with the bags. I'm wearing a dress, the green one, the first one I bought. I put it on this morning, forced myself to wear it, to travel. But whereas this dress used to fit perfectly, now it feels all wrong. Not only uncomfortable and scratchy but dirty. The fabric feels oily against my skin. A man brushes past, his sleeve against my arm, and looks me up and down. Before, this kind of thing didn't bother me. It even used to flatter me on the streets of New York, the lingering looks, the comments in passing. But all at once I feel uneasy. I look around. The station is full of men. Maybe I'm imagining it, but I think I see a quick glimpse of a woman disappearing through a doorway, her light-colored skirt and legs, and then there are only men. Their cuffs. Their pant legs and collars. They're all dressed exactly the same. Turning, milling nearer. I feel their breath closing in. They sense it, smell it, like dogs do, my fear. But they aren't dogs. They're infinitely more subtle, infinitely more terrifying—men.

We take the train out of Paris. The webbed archway of the station is carried out in skeins, the strands of wires that follow us as far as the suburbs. Soon we're in the countryside. There's the green of grassy banks, the rounded gray-green trees. Cows grazing. What look from a distance like low medieval towns. Arthur studies a map. He says the names of things. I can't follow. The map, laid out before us, makes no sense to me. I can't even remember where we're heading. Arthur goes to the bathroom. He tells me to remember where we're going in case the conductor comes by. He says it twice, three times. The conductor comes by, but I can't remember.

We go to Chartres. It's a blur, climbing up the hill. We walk along a wall. I remember the wall distinctly. The town is above, the cathedral on a hill. I'm not sure that any of this is true. I'm sure only of that wall. And then the feeling of climbing up the narrow streets, climbing up and up, the walls close, that close, high-walled feeling, a block of sky.

Wandering through the dark streets of medieval towns. This seems to happen again and again. The walls are rough against your hand. Every once in a while, a neck juts out, a leering stone face, it spits out water. The streets have no names. They're lined with sheer walls, rough, lichen-covered. It's mainly black lichen, but here and there a plant grows out of a crack, the luminous blades of yellow-green, the small sprouts of flowers from which yellow dust falls.

In the town, all the shops are closed. I want a sip of water, at least a sip of water. The sun is hitting against the stone. The square in front of the cathedral is full of birds. They're working on the cathedral. There's a marked-off space with drop cloths and tools. They're restoring the figures of the prophets in the doorways. Are those the prophets? I know nothing, nothing. I'm tired of asking. Arthur seems exasperated every time I ask. Moreover, everything I once knew, I doubt now. It all sounds false. The less I know, the more Arthur seems to know. He seems almost bullying with all he knows. The more fear I show of him, the more he seems to bully. Is it true, or am I imagining it? I can't be sure.

Even if I wander away slightly, if I go down one of the aisles in the cathedral while he's going down the central nave, I begin to feel some blood returning to my limbs. I can feel my cheeks begin to tingle. But this all drains away once we meet behind the altar. I had seen something I wanted to show him, but I can't remember what it was. He tells me things, points out things. Maybe it's that I'm trying so hard to listen, I no longer have energy left to hear. I nod and nod, but I haven't heard a word.

Stepping out of the cathedral into the bright light, I now like the thought of those dark, tall streets, the walls, the narrow plunge down the hill. But then there's the bus again, the train. It all feels so awkward, so complicated and jolting. We try to speak. He misunderstands me, then I don't hear him. He's reading something. I say I'd like to read it, too.

Whatever I say sounds cryptic, insufficient. I am, after all, counting the words. I try to construct carefully beforehand what I'll say. The idea, of course, is to say something remarkable but in the fewest possible words. If it's too long, a paragraph, I know I'll never get it out. He looks at me puzzled. My comments all sound artificial, strange. After a while, I give up altogether and begin simply repeating things he's said. Surely he can't find fault here. These are, after all, things he's said himself.

We stop in Aix-en-Provence. It's a garrison town. I see the soldiers in uniform out in the yard, practicing with their guns. There's a casino, quivering trees lining the streets, a fountain of chubby, stone fish rising up on their tails, spouting water. I remember nothing. A few images, that's all. The dark hotel room. What is the rest of my mind doing? It's shut off, wandering inside itself. The dark house, the shutters all down. Every once in a while, there's a crack. Light comes through. I peer out. I can see something, the lovely, chubby fish of the fountain, the marketplace on Sunday in the square. All the fruits and vegetables are laid out on tables. The sun hits them. Everything glistens. Arthur walks along, his face lifted.

"This is the first time I've walked in the sun in years," he says.

I'm stumbling along beside him. I try to imagine what he must be feeling. I put my face up, too, and try to feel the sun.

On the other side of the square is a clump of men. They're milling around, talking among themselves.

"Gambling," Arthur says, "the horses."

He seems to know everything, while I know so little; his experience is monumental. It's like walking in the shadow of a looming cliff, a towering stone wall. When I try to speak, my words hit against the wall. They peter out, mean nothing.

Another hotel. It's dark. I can picture coming in the doorway, the light from outside. It's like entering darkness.

We have sex. I black out in the middle.

"What happened?" Arthur asks.

I hear him dimly. But I don't answer. I lie there, relishing the darkness. If only I could stay here, never come to.

When I'm alone in the hotel room, I imagine Jasper knocking at the door. I'd have stepped out of the bath and would be lying on the bed, wrapped in a towel. "There you are," I'd say—no, no, don't say that! But I'd say it anyway—"There you are. I've been waiting for you."

We're on the train again. We pass under stone bridges, soft with moss. Then purple fields, yellow fields, mustard and lavender. The softness, the colors against each other, the way it all flows by. Looking out, for a moment, it's as if the windows have all opened, a whole wall of the dark house. I'm out in the air again, seeing everything. The dark house is left behind.

I remember reading once in a book of letters, a mother writing to her daughter: "Look at colors. There's great solace in colors." Watching the yellow and the purple and the many shades of green, the soft gray-green of the distant trees, the tender yellow-green of the wheat, the blue-green grass pushing up, the blades casting shadows on one another, I feel that it must be true.

Canal country, lock country. We're gliding along, through glimmering fields. The canals run lugubriously, a murky green, sometimes clearer. The boats move slowly. They edge up along the grassy banks, stop for the night. Occasionally, they meet head-on. One retires to the side. They squeeze by one another. The canals move sluggishly through the towns. Stone bridges cross them. Children fish. Then, between towns, there are stretches of loneliness. Nothing. Grass banks, fields. Here and there a lock house. A lockkeeper's family. Their houses are like boxes, government-built, pretty and plain, perched up just along the edge of the canal. In front of some are rows of delicate flowers, pink and blue, or small apple trees with misshapen fruit, delicious though and sweet. The locks inside look as old as the earth. They're covered with moss, dangling waterplants. All day the water creeps up and fills them, then creeps down. There's a rush at first when the water enters them, a roaring sound, the boat inside tossed sideways. Then the lock mouth is immersed in water itself. Everything smooths over. The water creeps in, muffled, from underneath. The boat rises slowly.

We've taken a circuitous route but are nearing the place we've been heading to all along, the editor's brother-in-law's house in a little village in the countryside, sitting there, hollow, waiting. Will we go crazy together in an empty house? At least when you're traveling, there's the changing landscape, the views out the windows, the bustle and confusion.

We're at the last train station before we reach our destination. It has a glass roof, glass and iron. What town are we in, what country?

Have we crossed any borders? I have no idea. Arthur steps off to buy tickets. There are different rows of counters; he has to figure out which one to go to. I look around. I look up at the board above my head that lists the times and destinations of the trains. I see on the board that there's a train to Avignon, and one to Paris.

A moment later, the Paris train is called. People start moving toward one of the tracks. A train has pulled up. I see its nose, its sleek sides. Around it is a hive of activity, people in black, gray, or navy blue, with black or gray bags. More and more figures disappear into the train. Again they call the train over the loudspeaker. The quay is nearly empty. A conductor in uniform peers out. Just then, a girl comes running through the station, in blue jeans, a small bag over her shoulder, hair streaking back. She's running for the Paris train. The quay is now empty. She's sure she's missed it. There's no way she'll get there in time. They've already closed the doors. She keeps running. I watch her, my heart beating fast. She runs faster and faster, reaches the first door. The conductor peers out, the door opens. She, without missing a beat, slips inside. I can't believe it, I'm so relieved. The quay is now empty. I look over my shoulder but don't see Arthur, then back at the quay and the Paris train. It's moving now. It's pulling out and away. I stand there, poised, watching it go.

The village is perched up on a hill. As we approach in the taxi, we can look up and see it. Below in the valley are vineyards, rows and rows of them. The valley dips. The vineyards follow it, cling to its curves. Along the sides of the road are trees, but there's something wrong with them. I notice this immediately. Their limbs have all been cut off low down, near their trunks. They look misshapen, grotesque. Instead of trees, they're just stumps. It looks like they've been amputated. I can't believe it. I want to tear my eyes away, but I can't.

The house is large. There's a doorway with a stone floor, then stairs up. It's nice. I remember the doorway, the stairs. Then a large space above, a loft-style bedroom, and a view, windows, overlooking the valley where the vineyards are. I block out the view of the cut trees with one hand so I don't see them, just the rows of vines.

Arthur unpacks his things. He's excited to be here, eager to get to work. He goes into the study, off the front stairs. He's occupied, he doesn't necessarily want me around. It's a relief. I unpack my bag, try to settle down to read. But I hear his footsteps in the study. I can't concentrate. Is he really walking that much? I'm in the living room, but then I go up into the loft where the bed is. The footsteps here are even louder.

I decide to go out and look at the town. I walk, head ducked if I pass anyone. Between the roadway and the buildings are tufts of grass. The town is built upward. A steep brown road leads to the top. The houses are stone, with tiled roofs, and lichen and moss on their walls. You peer in a gateway. There's a garden with fruit trees, small, but for a child it would be a whole universe. I see a girl in a doorway looking out. I'm peering through the fence. She stares back at me. I walk up farther. There's a church at the top. The day is very clear. I look at the vegetables in the church garden, peer into the church.

I take a different road down and come to a small square. There's a restaurant here. I plan to tell Arthur about the restaurant, casually. "There's a nice little restaurant in town. Maybe we should try it." But the words have already been manufactured. They're not real words, not my words anymore. He's sure to sense this, sure to be irritated as soon as I say them.

The house is silent when I get back. He's in the study. He must be writing. I don't want to disturb him. I try to read. There are some English books here. But when I sit down, I find it hard to concentrate. There's something going on in my mind, great activity, scratching, muttering, fumbling. There's not room enough for another world, like the world of a book, to take shape. There's no space, no light. Always in the past, reading was the one thing I could do to forget. Everything entirely. A new world would bloom up and I'd be off, sailing over oceans, walking over heaths. Now there's none of that. I stare at the words. They don't take shape, the letters jump. They leap like bugs. Nothing, they evoke nothing. I'm left in the dark with this muttering and scratching.

Days pass. We're in the house together. My fear of him, far from diminishing, grows. There are no distractions between us. I hear the creaking of boards, him approaching, I want to hide. He sees the fear on my face. He's confused, then angry. I can hardly sleep with him in the bed. I don't want to touch him. I edge away. I jump if he touches me, even in his sleep. But aren't we supposed to be in love? Wasn't that the idea? This is supposed to be a love story. I try to hug him, I force myself. I grip him too hard. He's uncomfortable, breaks free.

He's "he" now, not Arthur. He no longer has a name in my mind. But that "he" is great, looming large, like a wall. One afternoon he's waiting for me, naked in bed, when I come in from a walk. I see him, but too late. I'm already too close. I freeze, terrified. It's a wild sort of fear. Animalistic. I'm frozen, my eyes darting. He moves. I flinch away, though I'm far from the bed, a yard at least. "My God," he says, "what is it?" He looks down at himself, frightened and bewildered to have provoked such an effect.

The next afternoon, I open a bottle of wine. I have a glass. Then I approach him. He's on the couch, reading. Without the wine, it's unthinkable. But this way I can. I approach him without hesitating. He looks up. I'm near. I sit down. I start to caress him. I'm not even looking at his face. He lets the book fall. He lets me do this. With our clothes still on, just opened, we begin making love. I'm not thinking, I'm not seeing him, only moving and touching him. Then he reaches out and moves me. He shifts my hips, corrects me. Or that's what it feels like. My eyes fly to his face. I'm doing this wrong, like everything else. I try to move the way his hands told me, but instead of going smoothly, my hips jolt against his hands. I was beginning to enjoy this, but now I feel nothing. I must have that look of fear on my face again, but he has his eyes closed. Then he opens them. He glances up and sees it, my look. He stops moving, sits up. "Don't look at me like that," he says, as if betrayed.

I shrink to the side. He sits up and zips his pants again, buttons his shirt. The world crumbles. Devastation. He stands up. I've chased him off the couch. Now what? He goes downstairs. I wait on the couch, the world destroyed around me. I look over at the counter. The wine's still there. I have another glass. It soothes me. I picture the wreckage floating in the water, floating away. I picture myself on a couch, floating. The house is quiet. He's nowhere. I don't care where he is. I'm on my couch, floating. There's wreckage, water all around. An hour or so later, when he comes up the stairs on his way to the loft above, I watch him and see to my astonishment that he's just a person, distinct and separate, nothing more frightening than that. And it occurs to me how he, like me, may be suffering. I hear him get into the bed. He's taking a nap, I think, trying to comfort himself. Suddenly everything seems quite clear, our shared confusion and helplessness, as if we've gotten lost in the woods, both of us, and can't seem to find our way out.

Night falls heavily. I sleep on the couch. Midway through the night, I wake with a headache. I get up and drink a glass of water, then go back to the couch. I sink into it. I'm sleeping, really sleeping after nights of not. Day comes. I wake and hear him walking through the house. My heart starts beating rapidly. I'm frightened again. I peek up at him. I see his face as he turns in to the kitchen, his profile. I try to recover some of the understanding I had the night before, the vision I had of him as simply a person, but I can't. It's not there. With the arrival of morning, he's once again looming.

Not able to face him, I pretend to be asleep. Finally I can no longer stay still. I open my eyes. He's in the kitchen, making an effort. He suggests that we go to the restaurant in town for dinner tonight. What's he thinking? What's he planning? All day I worry. Does he want me to leave? Will he leave? How will I ever manage alone? I go out and walk down the line of vineyards, the stumped trees to my left. I don't look at them. I refuse to. The grapes are growing, green still. There are little wooden tendrils all along the vines. I step into the vineyards, looking over my shoulder, fearing that I may be caught by the farmer. What would he do? Yell at me? Hit me? I'm hidden between the rows of vines. I press my face into a flourish of leaves, close my eyes. Oh, to stay here and never return.

I walk back up the hill, as if fulfilling a sentence. Evening comes. We're going out to the restaurant. The thought fills me with dread. We're walking down the street, heading for the square. I let Arthur walk a bit ahead, as always. I'm plodding behind, a step or so. I feel as if I'm being led, an iron chain around my neck. Why all these images? These medieval tortures? I can't explain it. At the restaurant, we're sitting face-to-face. The light is bright. All eyes are on us, the outsiders, foreigners. It's everything I've feared.

"So," Arthur says. He folds his hands. I don't look up at his face. At last I do. Just a glance. I look down. His face in that glance looked stiff and still. He's not happy. I think it from afar. But my impression—what I feel—is that he's angry at me.

"I think we have to do something," he says. "I think you're unhappy."

So he *is* trying to get rid of me.

"I'm—happy," I say. "Or maybe right now—I'm not that happy, but I will be. I just need—to relax."

His look is pained. But his voice sounds annoyed. "I think it's more than that."

I look up at him suspiciously. What could he mean?

"I think it's too isolated here," he says. "Maybe, it occurred to me, we should go somewhere else, somewhere lively, to the seashore. Or maybe we should go back home."

He's trying. I can't quite believe it.

I wince. "I'm fine," I say, "I'll be fine here. You need to write."

"No, you're not fine," he says. "You're not fine at all."

I fall silent.

Maybe, I think later, it's because of the dream. People, it seems to me, always describe premonitions much too clearly, as if they understood them in the moment, when in fact they mean nothing without hindsight.

My dream, in any case, is wonderful. It isn't the feeling of a tree or that I'm like a tree. I *am* a tree. I wake up, it's dawn, and feel for a moment as if I'm standing on a hilltop in the light and wind. Then, once again, the dark door closes.

But several days later, I wake again at dawn. I slip out of bed, my heart beating quickly, but my mind quite clear. I gather all my things rapidly, soundlessly, and creep down the stairs. I'm still in my night-clothes. Arthur sleeps on above. I can hear his breath. I get dressed, fill my bag. I go to the bathroom and pack my things, then take a pear from the bowl. It's all so easy. I slip outside. I'm very careful with the door. It makes almost no sound, a tiny "shh" as it closes.

I'm in the street with my bag. I head down to the square, light-footed. There's no time to think, no time to lose. Not only because of Arthur but because of myself. I have to follow this one rippling cur-rent in my head. There are others, I know, that can pull me down. I have to simply keep riding this light one, at least until I'm far away.

I get to the square where the restaurant is. Outside is a taxi. I've seen it there before. Maybe, in some part of my mind, I've been regis-tering everything, preparing my escape all along. The driver isn't in the taxi. He's inside the restaurant having a cup of coffee. I go in. I go up to him, promptly. I find all the words I need in French. They're all there somewhere. I ask him if he'll take me to the train station. He nods, takes his last sip, and stands. Seconds later, we're both in the cab.

I sit forward on the seat, watching the road. I can't sit back, as if my sitting up will make us go faster. We drive down the road, past the vineyards, underneath the line of truncated trees. Then we turn onto a larger road, green on both sides. We're heading away from the village toward the town, where the market is, where the train stops. It's early morning, the mist rising off the grass, the cows in the meadows looking up at us.

The driver is silent. I'm grateful for that. We approach town. There's a stone wall alongside the road, lichen-covered; behind it, houses with small fruit trees in their yards. We enter the town. Everything's in stone, the houses, the streets, everything gray, with here and there patches of green, a square of yard, tufts of plants growing out of walls. A central square, then up farther beyond, the train station. Before it, another set of stumped trees, taller, their trunks speckled, the bark peeling, sycamores, yes, amputated sycamores.

The driver pulls up to the curb. I pay him and get out. I enter the station lightly, the door swinging inward. It's tiny inside. There's a wooden board with a list of trains. There's one to Paris, only not immediately. I have a little over an hour to wait. What if Arthur comes after me? I think. He won't. He'll never know. He'll think, if anything, I've gone out for a walk.

I buy my ticket and step onto the platform. I want to be out here, as near as possible to any passing train. If I see him, I hop on, I think, to any passing train, it doesn't matter. I'm also scared, of course, of myself. But I stay calm. I keep focused on the view across the tracks. The other platform and the awning there, empty. Behind it, more of the town, and then farther above, a soft hill rising. Fields, they must be. I see the dot of a figure crossing, turning, crossing back. The field is already plowed. I can see the dark grooves, even from here. He must be sowing, I think.

The platform is deserted for almost an hour. Then a few people arrive, a boy and his mother, an old man. The train comes. I get on. I step on, just like that. I take a seat by the window. The train is nearly empty. It jolts once, then smoothly pulls away. We're quickly past the town and in the countryside. The soft green hills, slow-moving streams.

The train picks up speed, glides swiftly. A girl running. I close my eyes, then open them, then close them again. A girl running, I see her, hair streaking back. The landscape passes swiftly, streaks, streams by.

CHAPTER 13

ROE IS TRAVELING, TOO. JESSE, HER BOY, SHOWS UP ONE DAY at her father's house. Her father's out at work. Jesse is casual. He says he was just passing through and thought he'd stop by to say hello. He got a job, earned enough money to buy a car. It's an old car, but it runs beautifully, he says. He turns at the door and points it out, sitting on the curb behind him.

"I'm in love with it," he says. "Look at the old girl."

The car is beaten down, low to the ground. Roe likes it, too. But she doesn't know what to do. He's standing in the doorway. He looks fresh and happy, changed.

"I've changed a lot," he says, as if he's heard her thoughts.

But should she ask him into her father's house? The thought frightens her. She edges herself outside instead, standing with him on the small porch.

"You drove all this way?" she asks.

He's proud. "I've been all over."

"And where do you sleep?"

"In the car," he says. He makes the motions of it. "You tilt the seat back."

They still haven't kissed. Roe looks out at the street. It's strange

not knowing how to behave. But she's happy to see him. She's looking at the street, but he's looking at her. She can feel it.

"You look so pretty," he says finally.

She flushes.

"Do you ever think about me?" he asks.

He looks so young and hopeful. He's trying to grow a beard, she
can see that, but only half successfully, the larger part of his chin still
completely bare.

Roe doesn't want to lie. "Yes," she says.

"You do?" he asks.

"Of course," she says, looking down.

"I think about you all the time." He's so brave, she feels, to say
these things, even knowing she might not say them back, might not
want to see him still. He's always been like that, always said things.
This is something she admires. Now he talks with great warmth,
describing how he lies in bed at night thinking of her so that he'll
dream of her once he's asleep. If he can't see her while he's awake, he
wants at least to be able to dream of her, to see her in the night.

"And I do, I often do. Sometimes, though, you're mad at me. Or
you're leaving, rolling out of a window. Once you did that. But even
if you're mad, I prefer to see you, at least to see you. Listen," he says,
"can we do one thing? You're not busy, are you? Can I take you for a
drive?"

Roe's father isn't coming home until later. It isn't that she's not
allowed to see anyone, or even to see boys. There's no fixed rule
against that. But there's something particular about Jesse, about her
father meeting him, that frightens her. Not that her father knows
anything about him. Of course she hasn't told him. But she feels sure

that her father will sense something as soon as he sees Jesse. And she fears that if he ever does find out the truth, that Jesse hit her, her father will kill the boy. Of this Roe feels absolutely sure.

She goes inside and gets her shoes, and they go for a ride. She knows this means something. It's a step in one direction. Yet at the same time it feels like such a simple, natural thing to do, and so refreshing after the monotony of her days.

They say almost nothing at first. Roe eyes him sideways. She feels really very happy, and almost shy, to be sitting here riding along with him. He looks at her, delighted. They drive around. She shows him things. He seems calm in a way he's rarely been before, as if he really has changed, gained some sort of mastery over himself.

Before dropping her off, he says he thinks he may stay in the area for a day or two, then head out to Texas. That's his eventual plan. He leaves her in front of her house. He just leaves her. She's expecting some sort of scene, even hoping for it, some sort of expression of desire or even desperation. Nothing. He leaves her calmly, almost casually.

"Can I come back tomorrow?" he asks.

She agrees. He doesn't kiss her. She can't believe it. Once he's gone, she's dying to kiss him. She falls back on the couch. She already can't wait for the next day, when he'll come again, so she can kiss him.

He comes back the next afternoon. This time she kisses him right away, taking his face in her hands. And from then on, he comes every day. He's lingering in the town. He lives out of his car, parked near the quarry. He bathes in the quarry. Roe washes his clothes at her house when her father's out. Things are growing dangerous. Roe feels it. There's the fear and the thrill that her father will find out. Suddenly her days are full of suspense. She and Jesse are sleeping together again, wherever they can, in the car, at the quarry, under the thick hanging leaves. They try to do it in the water. Once they even do it in Roe's father's house while he's gone. It's terrible, terribly forbidden. Roe pictures her father getting his gun.

One day Roe's father tells her that someone's seen her around town with a boy. Who is he? he wants to know. He wants to meet him. It's arranged that Jesse will come by the house.

They sit in the living room and have tea. Jesse is at his best behaved. Roe's impressed to see him like this. He leans forward eagerly as he talks to Roe's father, telling him all about himself. But Roe's father doesn't like him. Roe can tell. She knew he wouldn't. He senses these things. On one level, her father seems very rough. But he's extremely sensitive, intuitive, on another.

Roe and her father walk Jesse out to his car. It's evening. Then they come back into the house. They're standing in the front hall by the staircase. Roe's father has his hand on the banister. He looks down.

"I don't want you to see him anymore," he says.

"Why?" Roe asks, knowing why.

"I get a bad feeling about him."

"But I want to see him," Roe says.

Roe's father looks over her shoulder, avoiding her face. For a fraction of a second, he seems to waver. Then he sets his lips. "You won't see him anymore. That's final, as long as you're living in this house."

The next afternoon, when Jesse stops by, Roe comes out of the house with a small duffel bag. "Let's go," she says.

"Where?" Jesse asks.

"To Texas. Isn't that where you're headed?"

"Are you serious?"

Roe nods.

"What about your father? He didn't like me?" Jesse seems nearly brokenhearted.

"No, no, it's not that," Roe says. "I just want to go. I'm tired of being here."

"And your father?"

"I explained everything. I left him a note."

They're driving. It's a thrill. It's even more of a thrill than Roe had imagined, the windows all open, their hair blowing wild. They drive all day and then sleep in the car. They both have a little money saved, Jesse from his job earlier in the summer, Roe from working at the Bluebird Café. They eat in roadside places. This, Roe thinks, is better than anything. Why didn't she think of doing this before?

Jesse seems different, levelheaded, truly changed, as he'd said. Roe is impressed, she can't quite believe it; then the change begins to bother her. One day she decides to try to get a rise out of him by making fun of his obsession with the Catholics in Ireland. "You call yourself a Catholic? You're not Catholic," she says. "I've never seen you once go to church. Or say, or even think, anything Catholic."

He laughs it off. She gets angry. She can't believe he's laughing at her, remaining so calm. "What, have you reached some sort of nirvana?" she asks.

He laughs again. "No, it's not that. I just don't want to fight."

But Roe does want to fight. She does. The more she does, the more he won't respond.

"Maybe part of it," she says to me later, "part of the appeal was the intensity of his temper. Or at least the intensity of those moments when his temper showed itself. Maybe that was really part of what I wanted."

One day, when she provokes him, he does respond. They've been driving all day through the heat and dust. They stop at a motel, near a high-security prison. The room smells funny, like metal. Nothing works, the shower, the stove. The light flickers. Jesse is edgy in the old way. Roe could have chosen this moment to retire, back off. Instead she needles him. They fight, the light humming loudly above them. He lunges across the room. Her head and hair go flying. He's coming toward her again. She picks up a lamp. She's about to throw it at him, but can't. She drops it. This goes on. And then afterward, he blames her for starting it up all over again.

The fine pleasure of those early days gives way to madness. They're driving. They're fighting, slamming car doors, screaming down highways. Sometimes one person gets out of the car in a rage. The other drives off, then backtracks much later. They search for each other in tiny towns. Whoever is in the car creeps around, peering down back alleys, into diner windows and bars. At night they either get a motel room or sleep in the car. The motel rooms are perfect sets for fights. He drinks, gets heated. She goads him, doing her part. He hits her, throws her against walls, against bedposts. She has bruises in the morning, cuts, black eyes. Leaving in the morning light, they're both bashful. They skirt around, avoiding the front office, to get to the car. He goes in and pays. She's the girl with the bruised face who sits in the car. She can't believe that's who she is. It seems strange to her, almost inconceivable, so unlike anything she'd imagined for herself.

There's that waiting in the car as he pays. Then they're driving again, the countryside rugged and beautiful, long grasses, telephone lines. They ride in silence. There's nothing to say. He tries not to look at her. When he does look at her, he seems about to cry. Sometimes, instead of crying, he gets mad.

"You don't have any self-respect," he says with disgust.

It confuses Roe, the word "self-respect." Then she remembers. We'd talked about this. She clings to the idea. Is that what's missing, self-respect?

The bruises are also great weapons against him. All she has to do is sit there and be bruised. He feels terrible, he'll do anything. A moment later, though, she wants to hide them. He feels too terrible, the expression on his face too broken, pleading. She wants nothing in the world but for him to feel all right again.

They drive through the desert, dust rising, the underbrush silver. More motels. Always afterward, for a few days, he's sweet. They both are, lying in a motel room together in the darkness. The fan swirls above them. Roe, wide awake in the night, watches it, swirling the dark air above. They were just playing, pretending to be adults, and then a dark wave hit them. This is real life. Or is it?

"I'm not sure," Roe says later, "that that's real life. Or even at all the most interesting part."

But for the moment, they're terrified. Of each other, of themselves and the darkness swirling above. They have several days of sweetness or even a stretch of them. Then something else creeps in, at first just an itch. Irascibility. The thing mounts and hovers. For a moment it's very quiet. Then it breaks. He comes after her. She tries to make it to the door. She does try to escape. It's not that she doesn't.

All along, part of her tries to escape; another part hangs back. The scene repeats itself. There's something heightened about it, of course, a certain thrilling vein. Roe feels jolted, alive. The dullness comes afterward. Sitting in the car, Roe feels trapped. She wants to leave now, but can't. Not yet. Perhaps not ever, she begins to feel.

One morning in a diner she picks up the local paper and reads about a woman getting killed by her husband. Beaten and killed. That's how I'll end, she thinks, laughing. But her lip is swollen. It hurts to laugh.

CHAPTER 14

PARIS AGAIN. I HAVE A LITTLE OF MY GRANDMOTHER'S MONEY left. I don't know how long it will last. From the train station, I take a taxi to the university. I'll check in to that same hotel. The driver drops me off on the other side of the university; I walk around it and find the square of students. My bag is heavy, but I seem to be managing it. I approach the hotel and stop. What if Arthur comes after me? Shouldn't I go somewhere else? I walk on a bit farther up the narrow street. On one side is the wall of the university. On the other side, shops, a restaurant, and then I see it, a little hotel. I go inside.

My room looks out on a narrow street tripping up a hill. On the other side is the wall of the university. Students trail along it carrying their books. Although the wall throws a shadow, there are certain hours when there's light in the room. Above all, the room is mine. During the first few days, I hardly leave it. I'm tired, very, very tired. I get up and go out to bring back food, sandwiches from the bread store, fruits from a stand. I'm sleeping in a way I've never slept before, as if I'm diving underwater each time, plunging under as I drop my head down.

When I wake at last—that is, really wake—I feel weak. I go to the window. A boy student is wending his way along the wall. I watch him. He has dark hair, dark eyes, red cheeks. He's going down toward the square. Then a girl appears, coming up. I feel weak but more lucid than I have in a while. I sit by the window and watch the students walking up and down along the wall. After a day or two of this, I want to see more. I peer out along the edges of the window. From one angle, I can see the corner of the square. From the other, the little street going up, a rectangle of sky. Should I go outside and look? In my forays for food, I've hardly looked up. But now I want to. Do I dare? What happens if someone approaches me? Will I be able to talk? The fears hover like wings up near my heart, transparent, beating rapidly.

I put on one of my dresses with a button-down shirt over it, so the dress is mostly hidden, and go downstairs. I peek out the hotel doorway and walk to my left, toward the square of students.

I still feel many of the old fears lingering. A taxi passes. I'm going to jump, to throw myself under the wheels. The thought flashes through my mind. I move nearer the wall.

I go to a café. I hesitate between several, then walk in one. It's on the corner of the square by a larger street. When I order a cup of coffee, the waiter smiles. At me? At my French? Am I behaving strangely? I have no idea. I've lost all sense of myself. I'm not at all sure how I appear to other people. Do I look old or young? Pretty or not? Or something in between? Do I look devastated? Am I in the blossom of my youth? If only I could see how my image registers on other people's faces. But that means studying other people's faces, that means daring to look straight at them. No, I can't do that. It's too much for now. I'm much more comfortable just looking at things.

I linger in the café looking out the window, trying to get

accustomed to the world outside. I realize that I'm hungry and order a little something, an omelette with bread. Finally I get up and go out. Part of me wants to head straight back to the hotel, but the other part is curious. I look toward the larger street. Then I see a smaller street off the square, leading back between stone walls. I take it, it seems safer, Champollion. It's very narrow, no one's on it. It intersects at the bottom with another street that revives a dim memory. I've been here before, rue des Écoles.

I turn down the rue des Écoles, walking cautiously, looking all around. I stop to look in the shopwindows. I don't go inside. The windows are full of different things, sitting there quietly. In the lamp shop, there are lamps of all variations, small and thin or squat, with cloth shades, paper shades, tasseled shades, some very modern, long and thin, others antiques with their cords frayed. I feel as if I could stand here all day looking. Why? What's so pleasing? They're asking nothing, just sitting there. I pass a taxidermist's shop. Small animals and birds are crouched or perched on branches in the window. I look in another window full of shoes, row upon row. The uniformity pleases me.

The next day I go again to the rue des Écoles. I take the same path. I look again in the shopwindows. The following day, too. I don't want to go inside, to face someone and have to talk. The café and the waiter are enough. That's where I have all my meals now. They bring me what I ask for. The waiter no longer loiters or smiles at my French. I appreciate that, being left alone. I appreciate it so deeply I almost want to tell him. But no, that would bring on conversation.

I lose all track of time. One day I follow one of the little side streets all the way down to the river. The water rippling, the leaves rippling above. How could I have forgotten? Why didn't I think of it before? I'm peering down at the river from the street above. Alongside the water are the pale rounded stones, the elephant curves of the quay. I look from here—it's enough for today—and go back to my room. The next day I come and look again. People are strolling along the quay. Should I go down there, too?

Strolling along the quay, I keep my eyes fixed on the next set of steps so I can escape if I need to. Escape from what? I don't know exactly. It isn't clear in my mind. A man is approaching me. What should I do? Turn back? Veer off to the side? I look up to the street above. People are walking there, too, a couple. I have an idea. I wave up to the couple. Surely the man would never attack me if he thinks I have friends so nearby.

I begin to make it a habit to take a walk along the quay. I love watching the water and the rippling leaves. Sometimes I almost close my eyes as I'm walking. This way I can feel the breeze and hear the sounds of the water and leaves more clearly. At other times, though, I feel threatened, on guard. I look for the next set of steps. A moment later, this seems silly. I see how fine it is. People are leaning back on benches, sunning. Others, teenagers, are dangling their feet off the side of the quay. The water's far below. Someone ties up a boat on one of the large iron rings.

THE DAYS ARE EITHER GRAY AND RAINY OR WARM WITH SUN. I go out no matter what. My shoes get wet, then are stiff in the mornings. I cross one of the bridges from the mainland to the islands. The islands, I remember them, but only dimly, some cherub faces in a doorway. When I walked here before, I was looking down, clutching Arthur's arm. Now I look up. I explore the islands. Next I cross over a bridge from the islands to the other side of Paris. There's a street of rushing cars shooting diagonally back. I walk down it. I pass a red and gold café, a tobacco shop, a flower shop, then nothing more, no shops, no objects to look at, only a high stone wall. From behind the wall, I hear a stomping, then a snorting. I look up. There's a grated window. The strong, delicious smell of horse, locked away somewhere inside.

One day as I'm passing by a bookstore on the far side of the islands, I see a name I recognize on a book jacket in the window— Marie Loup. The cover is white, the print black. I go in to look. It's a hardcover. I turn it over. There's a small black-and-white photo on the back. Marie Loup, Madame Loup. It's her, I can't believe it. I look at the first page, in French, of course, but my French is coming back. The words, the sentences, all make sense. I buy the book. I walk around with it all day in my bag. Later, when I'm having dinner at the café, I take it out and read.

The sentences are simple, mournful. She uses the same words over and over again. It's the story of a girl growing up by a river. There's a lunatic asylum nearby. But it's not so much the story, though there is that, too, as the way it's told. The sentences stream by like a landscape out a window. I read over dinner at the café then go on reading in my hotel room late into the night.

Time ripples by, dreamlike. I go into a museum. I'm walking through the rooms when something catches my eye. I slow down and look closely. It's a room of Cézannes. There's a painting of a slow-moving river with a bridge over it and grassy banks. In the grass are the little white stars of flowers. I keep looking. Across the room is a painting of a hillside with gray-green trees, then another of a cathedral, it's Chartres. They're doing construction outside. That's what I saw, I think. The slow-moving river, the cathedral, the hillside and trees. Yes, that's it, that's exactly what I saw. I look around. There's a man in the room with me, in a corner, studying a canvas closely. I turn to him, I almost want to tell him, to marvel with him about how I, too, saw these things.

Out on the street again, I feel refreshed. It's a large street by the quay. There's a wind from the river, a light breeze, really. But then the cars go rushing by. My hair and clothes rise up, blowing wildly. I think of Roe. I stop in my tracks. Where is she? I absolutely have to call Roe.

I go back to the hotel and ask the man at the desk how to make a long-distance call. He tells me all the numbers, and I go upstairs and call. Roe's father answers. Roe's not here, he says. She went on a trip. She'll be back soon, he doesn't know when exactly, in a week or so. When I ask where she went, he pauses. "To see a friend of hers," he says. But his voice sounds funny. There's something wrong. Before I can ask more, he hangs up. I suddenly can't stop thinking of Roe. Where could she have gone? How could he not know?

The end of the week comes. I call again. Her father answers. She's still not there. That night I have a dream that she's died. I wake up seized with fear. I sit up, heart pounding. For a moment I think there's daylight out the window. I can get up, go out. But then I pull aside the curtain and see that it's the streetlamp. I look at the clock. It's only two in the morning. I have the whole night to go through. I lie there, waiting for the light. But what will it bring? What will the light change if Roe's dead? My body's very tired, but my mind keeps turning. What will I do, where will I go, if Roe's dead? The night drags on. When the first light appears in the sky, I go out to the café.

I watch from the café as more light fills the sky. I drink coffee. Then I come back and call again. The telephone at Roe's house rings and rings. I call her all that day. Now I'm certain she's dead. Morning and night pass, that long gray week. I call and call. I forget to be frightened of anything anymore. I pass without thinking from my room to the café to the street and back again. Surely it's my fault. How could I not have called before? I try to comfort myself. Maybe it's nothing. Maybe the family has gone to the seaside. I hold on to this thought for a little while. But then it plummets. I remember her father's voice on the phone, how strange it sounded. No, she's dead.

I force myself to eat when I can. One day I try to force myself to read, so that I can think of something else, even briefly. I take Madame Loup's book with me to the café. I've already read it once through. I decide to read it again. At first I can't. I struggle through a page or two. My mind won't hold the words. Then something breaks. The page clears. I find that I can. The sentences stream by, telling the story of the girl but also something larger, my story, the story of every girl and boy in the world. I sit there and read page after page.

Then I ask for some paper from the waiter, as much as he can give me, and I begin to write. I write what happened from the beginning, about Roe and how we met and Arthur and all that I lived on this trip. It's a great relief to simply write and write. I feel that I have all the words reserved within me. Not that I won't be able to say it better later, once I've read many things and practiced, once I've learned to write. This is the first version. To get it right will take years. For now these words are all I have.

When I run out of paper, I leave the café to go buy more. Back in my room, I go on writing, sitting by the window facing the university wall. The next morning I wake and write some more. I go on like this for ten days, until I have the whole thing, start to finish.

Then I go out and walk. It's late afternoon. There's something different about the way I'm walking. I feel different. My head feels lifted and very clear, as if I can see over the top edges of the buildings. If I understood music, if I could love it, I would say that as I'm walking, I hear an imaginary tune. It's mine alone, no one else hears it. Yet it expresses all I'm seeing, all I've lived, heard, and felt so far. I feel suddenly sure that if I listen very closely, one day I'll be able to sing it. Yes, that's what I'm thinking as I walk along, that one day, if I listen closely and practice hard, I'll be able to explain, as Madame Loup has, not only what I feel but what other people feel. The music will be mine, but if I can sing it, it'll be something more. And that's what it must mean, the image I keep seeing as I walk along, of that goat-like leap, that brain flight from the little figure that is myself—I see her ant-size, from afar, walking down the Paris street—to the rooftops. I clamber there, hang. Will I pull myself up?

A day or two later, I book my flight home.

CHAPTER 15

THE FLIGHT WAS SERENE. I FELT LONELY, NOTHING MORE.
But I clutched what I had written. I kept it with me. I had called Roe
several more times before I left, but the phone rang empty. I no
longer knew what to think, if she was dead or alive. As for myself, I
still felt unsure of everything, who I was, what I felt, what had happened to me. But I had what I'd written. That seemed concrete. I
could show that. The plane lifted and then landed. It was all a gliding movement, and I was inside. From the plane windows, I watched
the clouds rolling by. I'm alone, I kept thinking, very alone. And
where will I go now?

I considered calling my grandmother, going to her house. But
then there would be parties. There would be drinks and men. No,
there were certain things I kept thinking of, certain things I wanted
to see, the fruit trees by the garden, the water in the creek, the way it
changed colors, the wet morning yard.

I'm alone, I thought. And at my mother's, I'll be alone also. I
thought of the stretch of lonely days and again of Roe. Of speaking
to Roe. Who would I ever speak to again?

I went home. Returning along the road through the fields. I
remembered everything, everything minutely, it astonished me, the

ruts, the shape of the bank, each part of the woods, the place where the honeysuckle cast up its smell. And then the road curved. All this I'd forgotten. Forgotten utterly. How was it possible? I knew it so well. Now there was the drive. The yard spread out. I saw it. The fruit trees, the garden fence. Do we love things because we know them so well? Is it only that? No, I don't think so. There were other things I saw that I didn't love so well. But the fruit trees I loved. There they were, still growing, larger now, their limbs stretched farther.

I was amazed at how I remembered it all. It seemed somehow hurtful of me to have forgotten. The trees looked back at me, the bushes, the rocks. Even the shape of certain stones was familiar, and the curved pathway around the side of the house, the kind of pebbles that collected there.

I lay down upstairs in my old room. Lying there, I pictured clearly in my mind's eye the pear and walnut trees growing out in the yard. I pictured their roots drinking in water and the way they looked in winter, how their branches stood out against the sky.

I either lay down or I walked around and looked at things. One day, on my way in from the creek, I found my mother in her garden. We talked about the garden, what was growing this year, what she hoped to plant. But my mother and I didn't discuss what had happened on my trip. Did she not wonder? Did she not realize that something had changed? Maybe she did. But she didn't want to discuss it. I said once at the table, "Did you ever feel that you were losing your mind?" She looked frightened. She stood up and put the dishes in the sink.

I thought about Jasper. I couldn't not, when I was out in the woods, or passing by the barn. I remembered all the things we'd done together. I missed him, but I also wasn't ready to see him.

He'd heard from someone that I was home. He called. I told my mother to tell him that I wasn't there, that I'd left already. My mother looked at me. The next time he called—I was in the room—she did as I'd asked, told him I was gone. I heard her say it. She hung up the phone. I ran out into the yard. I stood under the fruit trees, sobbing uncontrollably. It felt as though I was crying for the first time in my life, as though I'd never cried before.

After a few days, I took out what I had written and worked on it some more in my room while my mother worked outside in her garden. But it was a waiting period, an interval. I was soon going back to school.

The days passed. The interval shortened. Like the time spent on a dock, on a platform, half living, mostly waiting.

I had spoken to Roe. She was alive.

"But just barely," she said. She laughed her light laugh. She had a real twang now. "I'll tell you," she said, "I have a thousand things to tell you."

"I do, too," I said.

BACK AT SCHOOL, THE LIGHT IS LOWER, SLANTED, AND GOLD along the edges of the leaves. I'm relieved to be in my own room again. I have all my things here. I've brought what I've written to show to Madame Loup. Roe hasn't arrived yet. I wait for her, pent up.

When she finally does arrive, I'm so excited I'm almost shy. She is, too. She has her old clothes on. Her things are in duffel bags, colored army green. I help her carry them up the dorm stairs. She, too, is in the same dormitory, the same room, as last year. Neither of us had requested a change. We didn't think of it. In our minds we hadn't imagined being back here again, not really. What had we imagined? Passing into the world, embarking on our lives.

We look at each other. School hasn't started yet. What should we do?

"Should we go into town?" Roe asks, almost laughing, not because it's funny but because we still can't believe that we're actually here.

We head down the hill, the cracked sidewalk, the houses up high on their porches. We pass the thrift shop and peer in. We'll go there later, we decide, if not today, tomorrow. We head for the diner. The main street, the policewoman, the empty lot full of weeds. In the diner, the soft-limbed waitress serves us. We tell each other what happened, or we try to. It's the first time around. We'll have to go back over it again and again.

"It was a feeling," I say, "of being drained of myself. And I couldn't speak. It was as if there was nothing left there to speak." I still feel uneasy telling it, even scared. But there's also a pleasure in trying to explain.

Roe is watching. I tell her how I dreamed that she died.

"When was that?" she asks. I try to think back. Neither of us is very clear about the dates. Late July? August? "It was about then that I actually did almost die," Roe says.

We've finished our coffee, are out and walking. We've come to the place where the town peters out, beyond the shopping center. There's the river and the mill. Roe turns as she's walking and shows me a scar under her lip.

"My God," I say, "is that from a fight?"

She nods, then shakes her head, as if baffled at herself. We stop on the bridge. "My father came after us," she says. "In his pickup. He looked for us for weeks."

I'm remembering how, after I'd talked to him once, the phone just rang and rang.

"He found us. I was sitting in the car outside a motel. I had bruises and everything. Jesse was inside. My father came over. He knocked on the window, then opened the door and took my hand, very gently, and led me over to his pickup truck. I followed automatically. I noticed that he had his gun on the seat of the truck, but he wasn't carrying it. Then he went back and got my bag from the car." She's looking down at the river, the gray furling water. "Jesse came out of the motel office then. I saw him look at Pa. But Pa wasn't looking up, he wasn't looking around at all. I think he was trying not to see Jesse. Pa came back over to the truck. Then Jesse saw where I was. He looked at me through the windshield. I thought he was going to come over, start something. But then Pa climbed in the truck. He looked up through the windshield. This is it, I thought, he's going to see him. But Jesse must have ducked back out of sight. He wasn't anywhere. Maybe he was relieved, too. He wanted it to end but couldn't make it. He knew, like I did, that this was our chance. Pa and I drove in silence nearly the whole way home."

The gray water furls. Along its edges are the first wet leaves falling. We turn and make our way back up through the town, along the little side streets. We pass Jesse's friend's house, the back porch with the pink cushions. I'd forgotten about it but now remember clearly, the place from which Roe ran.

[227]

"Where is he now?" I ask warily, not wanting to sound scared or to make her scared.

"Jesse, you mean?" Roe says. "I don't know." There's a quick nervous flash in her eyes, then it's gone. "I doubt that he came home."

We keep walking, up the back way, passing the inn, then the chapel. There's the chapel bench, deserted. We go over to look at it, then continue on across the Green.

Under the copper beech tree, the sun is slanting lower. We look over the graveyard. Roe walks between the stones. I peer very closely into the beech tree's bark. There's a whole universe inside, ants trundling up and down the wrinkles, transporting in tandem an insect's wing. I turn my back and slide down the trunk until I'm sitting. Roe comes over.

"Sometimes I wonder if trying to attract men isn't really a dead end," I say.

Roe's still standing. "What do you mean?"

"Well, just that. I'm just wondering if it really doesn't lead anywhere, and, I mean, least of all to a man."

Roe laughs. She squats down. "Do you picture your life with a man?"

"Well, yes, that's what I'd like eventually. If I'm able to be with one."

"I would, too," Roe says, "if I can." She pauses. "Can you even picture your life?"

"Well, no, not really. At least not in any ordinary way."

"Oh, it can't be ordinary," Roe says. She stands again. "I won't have an ordinary life."

"Well, what then? It has to be interesting?"

"Yes, interesting, that's the word. Don't you agree?"

I nod, watching her. She's picked up a stick. She's walking around the beech tree, the stick in her hand. "And there's another thing I've decided," she says. "From now on I want to enjoy things."

I look at her, astonished. "Can we?" I almost whisper it.

"Can we what?"

"Enjoy things?" I say. "I mean, I think I thought we were supposed to *experience* them."

"Can't we do both?"

I feel my mind being irrigated outward. "I guess so," I say. The idea never occurred to me.

Roe shrugs. She smiles. "I don't see why we shouldn't try."

I look at her. I think of those shoots of grass growing up in the barren lots of the town, or those sprouts of green pressing out of the stone walls in the medieval villages. Is there a part of us, I think, that sprouts on its own, regardless of the circumstances, simply breaks free?

That evening, before curfew, we go out to sit on the chapel bench. The night air is cool. Before us are the heavy pines. The wind blows through them.

Life, we've agreed, has definitely started.

"But," we ask each other, "what will happen? What do you think will happen now?"

ACKNOWLEDGMENTS

Grateful acknowledgments go to my mother and my father and to my siblings, Leda, Jake, and Kyle; and to the friends who have served as readers and models: Jane Brodie, Danielle Brunon, Eva Marer, Eliza Minot, Lauren Mueenuddin, Ruby Palmer, Evie Polesny, Gwen Strauss, and to the memory of Elizabeth Wood. I especially wish to thank Mary Gordon, invaluable teacher and friend, and Frances Coady and Sarah Chalfant, for their staunch support of this book. Additional thanks go to Don McMahon. Lastly, but also crucially, I'm grateful to the people who gave me places to write: Star Gifford, Henry Greenewalt, Deborah and Guntram Hapsburg, Katherine and Jim Ingram, Claudia Ceniceros, and Horacio Kaufmann, Lauren and Tamur Mueenuddin, Clover and Nick Swann, Mary Swann and Josh Brumfield, and Yaddo.